YANKEE BELLES IN DIXIE

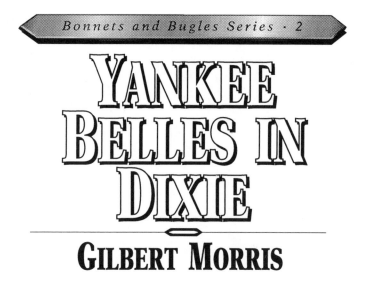

Bonnets and Bugles Series · 2

YANKEE BELLES IN DIXIE

GILBERT MORRIS

MOODY PRESS

CHICAGO

ISBN: 0-8024-0912-1

5 7 9 10 8 6

Printed in the United States of America

To Dixie—who has brought sunshine into my life

Contents

1. Leah's Plan   9
2. A Matter for Prayer   18
3. Rebel in Washington   30
4. A Good Yankee   39
5. Letter from Richmond   51
6. General Lee Gets Whipped   59
7. A Beautiful Spy   69
8. General Forrest Saves the Day   79
9. God Will Take Care of Us   85
10. Richmond   95
11. Sarah's Admirer   108
12. Lieutenant Lyons Smells a Rat   117
13. The Valley Campaign   127
14. Under Arrest   135
15. A Brief Trial and a Quick Verdict   147
16. A Gift from Heaven   157

1
Leah's Plan

Leah—don't move!"

Leah Carter had stepped halfway over a rotten log in the woods, but at the sound of Jeff Majors's voice she froze where she was. At the same instant she heard a buzzing that made her blood seem to run cold. With her foot half over the log, she lowered her eyes to a diamond rattler thick as a man's wrist and poised to strike. Its needle-sharp fangs were white, and its rattles blurred as they sounded their dire warning.

"Don't move!" Jeff whispered again.

Leah longed to turn and run, but she knew that the striking snake would catch her in the leg if she tried that. She heard Jeff to her left and wanted to cry out to him to be careful.

She felt the sun beating down on her head as she stood rigid in position.

Suddenly Jeff sprang into her line of vision. He struck at the snake with a large stick, shouting, "Get back, Leah!"

Leah leaped backward and in her anxiety sprawled full length on her back. She scrambled to her feet and saw Jeff still thrashing at the snake with all his might. "Be careful, Jeff! Don't let him get you!"

Jeff straightened up and turned to her, his face pale, and said in a voice not quite steady, "I guess that'll take care of him!"

Now that the danger was over, Leah suddenly felt sick. Her knees were weak and trembling. When Jeff dangled the snake over the stick, she cried out, "No, I don't want to see him!" She walked unsteadily away and leaned against a tall hickory. Her shoulders began to shake, and she put her head against the rough bark trying to hold back the tears.

Jeff dropped the snake at once and came to stand beside her. "Aw, Leah," he said uncomfortably, "don't cry. It's all over now." When she did not move, he tentatively put a hand on her shoulder and turned her around. Looking down at her, he muttered, "That was pretty close, but we made it all right."

Jeff Majors had the blackest hair possible and eyes so dark he was called the Black Majors by some of the family. Tall for his age and looking older than his fourteen years, he had large hands and feet. There was a look of durability about him. He wore a pair of worn tan trousers and a faded checked shirt, both somewhat small for him.

Leah pulled herself together, swallowed hard, and looked up. "You saved my life, Jeff. He—he would have gotten me for sure!"

"Well, I'm glad you didn't step on him. They're bad business."

Leah was sobered by the experience. "I could have died," she whispered. "You never think about such things until something like this happens."

"Sure. I reckon it pays to be careful in the woods—but when you're stepping over a log you can't always see what's on the other side."

* * *

10

Jeff looked down at Leah, thinking how pretty she had gotten in the last year. Today she wore a pair of faded blue overalls that had once belonged to her brother, Royal, but somehow she looked nice in them. One thing they had in common was their birthday—June fifteenth—but she was one year younger than he was. He admired her green eyes and blonde hair, now falling down her back, but to cover his embarrassment he said, "Well, you would've done the same for me."

"I don't know if I could have." Leah turned, and the two walked slowly along the forest path.

When they reached an opening in the trees, they paused and looked down into the wide valley. "I sure got lonesome to see that house of yours when I was gone to the army," Jeff murmured. He studied the Carter home, then lifted his eyes further. "Can't see our place from here. I missed it too— thought of it every day."

"Someday you'll all come back," Leah said softly. "The war will be over, and we'll all be together again just like we used to be."

The Civil War had shattered the little town of Pineville, just as it had other towns all over the country. Dan and Mary Carter, Leah's parents, had stood for the Union, but Jeff's father, Nelson Majors, had been Southern born. He had taken his wife and two sons South, settling in Richmond. Jeff's mother died soon after their arrival, bringing a new child, named Esther, into the world.

Looking down, Jeff thought of how it had been when they were growing up together.

Leah asked suddenly, "Do you have to go back and be a drummer boy, Jeff? Can't you just stay here until the war is over?"

"Why, I can't do that! I've got to be with my pa and Tom."

"But—but your father's in prison in Washington. He's not in Richmond."

Jeff's lips made a thin line, and he nodded curtly. "He won't be there for always. He'll get exchanged or . . . or . . ." The thoughts that ran through his mind disturbed him. His father had been taken as a prisoner of war at the Battle of Bull Run, and since that time Jeff had thought of little else except how to free him. Leah seemed to see that he was troubled. "Well, in any case, we've got Esther here. We'll take good care of her."

The Carters had volunteered to take the baby since Nelson Majors was in the army and had no way to care for a child.

Abruptly she looked at him and said, "Jeff, you know what I heard one time?"

He looked down at her curiously. "You hear a lot. What is it this time?"

Leah pursed her lips and looked thoughtful. "I read somewhere that if someone saves your life, you belong to that person somehow."

Jeff grinned. "Well, I guess you belong to me then. That means I get first helpings at the table tonight—and you have to wash all my clothes while I'm here."

Leah was more serious. "You always get first helpings—but I'll never forget how you jumped in there and killed that old rattler!"

"Oh, shucks, Leah, that was nothing." Jeff shrugged. But he was pleased with the way she looked at him. "I'm glad that I was there. I wouldn't want anything to happen to you. You're my best friend, aren't you?"

She smiled instantly, her teeth looking very white against her tanned face. "Yes, we'll always be best friends."

Jeff was shy in many ways. Although he and Leah had been best friends for a long time, he somehow felt embarrassed to talk about it. "Come on, let's go see old Napoleon."

They walked quickly down the path, emerging finally at a bridge that spanned a sparkling stream. Leaning on the rail they watched the small minnows sparkle in the sunlight. Occasionally a fish would break the water, and Jeff said wistfully, "I wish I had a line here. I'd catch some of those bass."

"I don't see old Napoleon though."

"He's a pretty smart fish, and I caught him once. So I don't think he's going to be dumb enough to get caught again."

Jeff remembered. They had been at this very bridge when word came that the North and the South were at war. That had been the beginning of hard times for them both.

"That was really something when you caught old Napoleon," Leah said quietly.

Old Napoleon was a huge bass, legendary almost, that had been able to avoid being caught for years. But Jeff had snagged the huge fish on his last visit and managed to get him to shore.

"You let him go, Jeff. I never did really know why you did that."

Jeff traced his initials on the wooden rail with his forefinger and was silent for a moment. Finally he said, "I guess I just like things to stay where they are. Everything's changing so quick. When I was in the battle at Bull Run, for some crazy reason I thought about Napoleon. We don't have a home here anymore, but I thought, *Well, as long as old Napoleon's there, not everything will change.*"

He thought again to the time he had pulled the thumping fish in, how he'd stared at him, then bent over and loosed the hook and let him go free. "Some of these days," he whispered, "when the war is over, I'll come back, and we'll catch him again, Leah."

"I don't know—I don't think I could eat old Napoleon. That would just be like eating Delilah." Delilah was the hammer-headed tomcat that dominated the Carter household.

Both of them laughed at the idea of eating Delilah, then they turned toward the house. On the way they stopped to look at several bird nests. For years they had collected wild bird eggs until together they had the best collection in the county. Leah had taken it when Jeff moved with his family.

"Look, Jeff, there's that tree where we got the wren's egg. Do you remember that day?"

Jeff stared up at the branches and thought for a moment. "And that's the day my brother Tom and your sister Sarah parked under it in the buggy." He smiled. "I sure felt bad about eavesdropping on them."

Tom Majors had been courting Sarah Carter before the war began. They were very much in love. Jeff only too well remembered perching in the tree with Leah when their buggy pulled up. Tom demanded to know why Sarah would not marry him. She had said it was because Tom may soon be fighting for the North but her brother Royal would fight for the South. "What would it be like if I married you—and you killed my brother—or he killed you?"

Thinking of this, Jeff shook his head. "Things sure have gotten mixed up, haven't they?"

Tentatively, Leah touched his arm, drawing his eyes around to her. "One day it will be all right. The war will be over, and Tom and Sarah will get married. And Esther will grow up, and you and your father will come back and live in Kentucky again."

"You really believe that, Leah?"

"Yes!"

Jeff examined her face carefully. "I'm glad you do. Sometimes I doubt it—but I hope you always believe it, Leah."

When they got within a hundred yards of the house, Jeff suddenly halted and took her arm. "I'll be leaving here soon."

"Oh, *don't* go back to the war—you could get killed!" Leah pleaded, looking up at him with alarm in her eyes.

"Well, I'm not going back to the army right now."

"Where are you going then?"

Jeff pulled off his straw hat and ran his hand through his black hair. He bit his lip. "I'm going to Washington—to see my father."

"Why—you can't do that!" Leah exclaimed. "You're in the Confederate Army. You're a drummer boy—not carrying a gun—but I don't think that matters!" She shook her head so that her blonde hair swung over her back. "You can't do it, Jeff! You'll get caught, and they shoot spies!"

"I don't care—I've got to do it!"

She stood there arguing with him.

Finally, when he said, "I'm going, and that's all there is to it," and she said, "You are the most stubborn boy on the face of the earth!" Leah seemed to have a sudden thought.

"Well, you can't go alone," she announced. "You can go with me and Pa." Jeff stared at her. "What do you mean?"

"Why, now that Pa's a sutler, you know we follow the Union Army everywhere, selling them things. The army's just outside Washington, and Pa said last night we're leaving soon to take care of the soldiers."

Dan Carter had decided that it was God's will for him—even though he was not in good health—to follow the Northern army and sell supplies to the soldiers. In addition to the usual tobacco and paper and thread, he carried Bibles and tracts, which he distributed to the lonesome soldiers of the Army of the Potomac.

Jeff shook his head stubbornly. "No, that wouldn't be right. You both might get caught. Then we'd all three get shot."

"We won't get caught."

Jeff knew she was almost as stubborn as he was.

For a time she seemed to be thinking hard. Finally her eyes began to sparkle. "You can be our helper," she cried. "You don't look like a Southern spy. Just wear those old clothes you've got on, keep your mouth shut, and nobody will ever know but what you're just a helper."

They talked excitedly, and by the time they got back to the house and went to find her father, Leah had already thought of a plan. She explained it carefully to her father.

Daniel Carter was a thin man with a rather sickly look and faded blue eyes. He listened, his eyes on the two of them, his mouth firm under a scraggly mustache. He had been badly wounded in the Mexican War and could not join the army now, but he wanted to serve his country. When Leah was finished, he nodded slowly. "Well, I think that may be the thing to do." He cut off Jeff's protest by saying, "You don't know this young lady like I do, Jeff. When she gets her mind set on something, she's as stubborn as a blue-nosed mule!"

"Pa, don't say that!" Leah exclaimed. "I'm not a bit like a mule!"

"Well, you're a lot prettier than one." Her father smiled. "But I still say you're just about as stubborn." Then he turned back to Jeff. "We'd better do it that way, Jeff. I know you're worried about your pa. You can go with us, and we'll see if the Lord will help us get to see him."

Jeff swallowed hard. The kindness of this family was more than he ever bargained for. When they had agreed to take his newborn sister, Esther, for as long as necessary, he'd thought they were the finest people in the world. Now he knew so!

"Thanks, Mr. Carter. Me and Pa and Tom, we won't ever forget you for this!"

2

A Matter for Prayer

Mama, I think Esther's the prettiest baby in the whole world!" Leah was holding Jeff's baby sister, making dimples in her rosy cheeks, and stroking her fine blonde hair.

Mrs. Carter stopped folding blankets and smiled over at her daughter. "You love all babies. You never saw an ugly one in your whole life."

"An ugly baby?" Leah was shocked. "Why, Ma, there's not any such thing!" She swung the child around in her arms and stuck her finger in the creases of her fat neck. "You're just the prettiest one, now aren't you?" she cooed.

Her sister, Sarah, sitting across the room churning, didn't break her stroke as she smiled at the pair. "I wish you did all your other work around here as well as you take care of Esther."

Sarah was a beautiful girl with dark hair and blue eyes. She had an oval face and a beautiful creamy complexion. However, she had not been as lively since the war started—especially since Tom Majors had left to join the Army of Northern Virginia.

But now she seemed to shake off the sadness that had come to be almost habitual and found a smile. "I thought you and Jeff were going to go trot lining."

"We are. I'm supposed to meet him down at the river." Leah put the baby into the cradle her father had made and ran her hands once more over the silky hair. "I'll be back, but you'll be asleep. I'll see you in the morning, Esther."

Leah's younger sister, Morena, was standing beside the cradle. She was eight years old with dark hair and powder blue eyes. She was pretty, but her mind had never developed.

"You take care of baby Esther, Morena," Leah said, hugging the younger girl. "I'll bring you a fish when I come back—all right?" She got no answer. She never did. However she did get a smile from Morena.

"Don't you fall in the river and drown," her mother said sternly.

* * *

Mrs. Carter folded the last blanket as Leah ran out of the room. Then she said to Sarah, "She's enjoyed Jeff's visit so much. They've always been such great friends."

Sarah continued to churn. "I hate to see him go back. Leah will miss him, almost as much as I—"

Mrs. Carter looked up quickly. "As you miss Tom?"

"Yes. I sometimes don't think I can stand it, Mother! He can be killed any day." She sighed and made a few strokes with the churn handle. Then she asked, "Do you think this war will ever be over?"

"All wars are over, sooner or later—and the good Lord will take care of Tom—and Royal too. We'll just have to keep praying."

* * *

Leah ran up to her room and put on her faded overalls. They were ragged and patched, but they

19

were comfortable. It would be cold on the river, so she grabbed a blue woolen sweater. Stopping suddenly before the small mirror on the wall, she looked at herself, then shook her head. "You giant you, why can't you be small like other girls?"

Leah saw herself as a giantess, and her mother had a time with her when she began stooping. "Leah, be as tall as God made you!" she'd said.

Remembering her mother's words, Leah straightened her shoulders involuntarily. She picked up an old black felt hat that had belonged to Royal, then dashed out the door.

The sun was far down in the west, throwing its red beams over the valley as she ran along the road. Already she could hear the night birds calling softly.

When she reached the river she saw a flickering fire and Jeff Majors sitting beside it, feeding sticks into the blaze.

"I've been waiting for you. We've got to get that line out before it gets dark."

"I'm ready."

"What've you got in your sack? Something to eat, I hope!"

"I knew you'd be hungry—you always are. Anyway, Royal's coming later," Leah said. "Right after dark. He's going to be our chaperone."

"Chaperone! What's that?" Jeff demanded.

"Oh, kind of a baby-sitter for boys and girls like us."

"Well—" Jeff shrugged "—maybe he'll be some help running the lines. Come on, let's go get the trot line out."

They clambered into the twelve-foot-long john boat. Built out of cypress, it would float even if full of water.

Jeff shoved off with a paddle. "I know a good place," he said. "We're going to catch more fish tonight than you've ever seen, Leah!"

He paddled toward a bend in the river, then got out his long cord. He tied it to the base of a small tree, then paddled across the river, letting the current take the boat a hundred yards downstream. There he tied the other end to another sapling. "Now," he said, "let's get the hooks on. You pull the boat along, and I'll tie them."

"All right. And I'll put the weights on too."

Leah loved trot lining. She had learned how from Jeff and her father when she was just a child. As they moved along the line, Jeff took hooks attached to twelve-inch strings and tied them to the heavy line about six feet apart. Leah's job was to attach an iron weight every twenty feet to keep the line on the river bottom.

They accomplished the job quickly, and when they got to the other side, Jeff said, "Now, you can do the fun part—baiting the hooks."

Leah turned up her nose. "That bait stinks. I hate that job!"

"You should have stayed home then." But Jeff grinned. "Catfish bait's supposed to stink. That's what makes them bite. But I'll do it. You pull the boat along."

Glad to get out of the baiting job, Leah hauled the boat slowly while Jeff baited every hook.

When they got to the other side, he put the top back on the bait can. "Now, we'll wait an hour. Let's go back to the fire."

As soon as they sat down, Jeff said, "I'm hungry. Let's eat!"

"We just got here!" Leah said indignantly. "You'll be hungry at midnight."

"I don't care. I'm hungry now. What's in your sack?"

Leah picked up the large bag, reached inside, and pulled out a smaller package. "Funnel cakes." She grinned broadly. "If you're good, you can have some."

"*Funnel cakes!* Gimme!" Jeff cried and took one from her hand. He bit into it and chewed slowly, closing his eyes. "Nobody can make funnel cakes like your ma. I wish I could take these back to camp with me—these and about a thousand more. They wouldn't last long with all those hungry soldiers though."

Leah took a funnel cake for herself and sat back and nibbled at it. "Tell me about the army, Jeff. What's it like?"

"I've already told you everything."

"Well, tell it again," she urged. "You don't know what it's like being stuck at home and the war's going on and we don't know anything. Tell me, Jeff."

Jeff took a bite of cake, chewed on it thoughtfully, then began. He told what it was like to be a drummer boy learning the different signals. "The troops, they couldn't go anywhere without us. We tell them when to charge, when to rally on the flag, when to go to the right or the left, when to retreat."

"You have to be awful close to the fighting then, don't you, Jeff?" Leah said. "Aren't you afraid?"

"I was only in one battle, but I was plenty scared that time, with bullets flying everywhere. I guess I was thinking most that I couldn't show the white feather. I couldn't let Pa or Tom see how scared I was—or the lieutenant. But I reckon all of us felt that way when we charged across the field."

Leah hesitated. "What was it like—to see people killed?"

Jeff swallowed the last morsel, and a moody look crossed his face. "I hated it," he said simply. "Seemed foolish to me. There was one fellow not much older than me. Well, just before the battle he told me how he was just about ready to get married. He was just in for ninety days—just wanted to see the battle."

The fire crackled, blowing sparks upward into the darkness where they seemed to mingle with the stars that were coming out overhead.

Jeff looked thoughtful and sad. "His name was Tim O'Reilly. His girl's name was Julia. He'd known her all his life, and they were planning a big wedding. He was going to get a little piece of land, he said, as soon as he got back to Alabama." He took up a stick and poked the fire. "He never made it though."

"I wish you didn't have to go back," Leah said again.

The two sat for a while, and then he said abruptly, "Tell me about being a sutler. What's that like?"

"Oh, it's not bad, not like—not like being in the fighting. We stay way behind the lines. The men come, and they buy paper to write letters, and they ask for tobacco and stamps and all sorts of things."

She continued to tell him about following the Army of the Potomac, and finally she lifted her head. "Listen, somebody's coming. Royal, I guess."

Sure enough, Royal Carter emerged from the darkness and came to the fire. He was nineteen and not tall but thick and strong with blond hair and blue eyes. He wore a ragged mustache and sideburns and was called "The Professor" by the men of his regiment because he had been to college.

"Well, how many fish have you caught?"

"Just waiting for you to go run the lines the first time, Royal," Jeff said. "Haven't heard any splashing, though, so maybe we ought to wait a while. Sit down and have something to eat."

Royal sat down and took some of the funnel cakes that Leah offered him.

Jeff had always admired Royal. He was the smartest man Jeff knew. He was his brother Tom's best friend, and the three of them had hunted together and fished together for years. At times, when Tom would have left Jeff at home, Royal would say, "Aw, let him come with us, Tom," which had endeared him to the younger boy.

After they had talked for a while, Jeff said, "Let's go run the lines now. We can all three get in the boat. You can pull us across, Leah, I'll take the fish off, and, Royal, you can bait up."

"No—" Royal shook his head "—I'll take the fish off, and *you* bait up. I don't want to get that bait all over me. It stinks too bad."

Jeff laughed, "You Carters are mighty fine folks —can't get your hands in a little fish bait. Well, that's OK. Us working folks will take care of that."

Leah got in the prow of the john boat, Royal positioned himself on the middle seat, and Jeff got in the stern.

"All right, Leah, haul us across," Jeff said.

Leah took the line up and began to pull the boat across the river. She got to the first hook and said, "Something got the bait."

"Rats," Jeff said. "I hope it's not going to be nothing but a bunch of bait-stealers tonight." He reached into his bucket, picked up a piece of bait, slipped it on the hook. "Let's go."

The first three hooks were bare, and Royal and Jeff baited them again. And then Leah cried out, "There's something on this one!"

"Watch out now! Let me get him!" Royal yelled. He always got excited when a fish was on the line, and as Leah drew the boat past the fish, he pulled it up saying, "A good one! Must go three or four pounds!"

"What kind is it?" Jeff asked. "Bullhead or blue channel?"

"Bullhead. Still good to eat though." Carefully Royal put his thumb in the fish's mouth, avoiding the spines that stuck out on each side of the broad head and out the top of the skull. The spines were poisonous and could cause painful wounds. He removed the hook, slipped the fish onto a stringer, and dropped it over the side. "OK, bait this one up."

Jeff slipped the bait on the hook and complained, "All the fun in this is catching the fish. I get to do all the work, and you get all the fun."

"When you get to be an old man like me, you can take the fish off," Royal teased.

Jeff knew Royal felt a real affection for him though and was glad the two of them happened to be home at the same time.

They moved slowly across the line, taking four fish off, three or four pounds each. And then, when the hooks were all baited again, they went back to the fire.

Royal said, "We got to do better than this." He sat down and reached into the sack. "Let's eat some more funnel cakes."

They sat eating cakes and listening to the night sounds. It was August and hot, but the wind off the river was cool, and they enjoyed it. Three times they ran the trot line. In between times, they talked as they sat around the fire. Once Leah and Jeff stretched out and slept for an hour.

Finally, at three in the morning, Jeff said, "I guess we got enough fish. We better go in, I reckon."

Royal, leaning back against a tree, said, "I wish Tom were here."

Jeff looked at him quickly. "Me too. We've sat around lots of campfires, haven't we, Royal?"

"Sure have." Royal stared into the fire thoughtfully.

Silence surrounded them, and they heard far away the sound of a coyote wailing at the moon. Finally Royal said, "He's all right, isn't he?"

"I guess so. He was when I left—but you know how it is, Royal." There was fear in Jeff's voice, and uncertainty.

Royal said, "You worry about him, I know. I do too."

* * *

Back at the house, about dawn, Jeff and Leah went to an outside table to clean the fish. He was wearing a pair of old faded overalls, and a slouch hat was shoved back on his head.

"Royal's worried, isn't he?" she asked him. "I can tell."

"I guess everybody is. This war's crazy—brothers shooting at brothers! There's Royal on one side

26

and my brother on the other side. The best friends that ever were—and now they might have to kill each other." He reached down, took the tow sack, and spilled the catfish into a pail. The fish thumped wildly about.

Jeff had dressed many catfish, and he did it quickly and efficiently, using a pair of pliers. When one was clean, he threw the trimmings into a small bucket and the pink body of the fine fish onto the table.

Then he said to Leah, "I can't seem to believe it's going to come out all right. There's my father in jail, and we hear the prisoners die by the hundreds in those prisons."

"Jeff, you can't think like that," Leah protested. She watched as he picked up another fish moodily and began cleaning it. "You've got to remember that God is going to answer our prayers. He'll take care of our men in His own way."

"I don't know about God anymore."

Leah reacted to his words as though struck. "Why, Jeff, you know God's good!"

He turned, holding the pliers in his left hand so tightly that his fingers were white. "If God's so good, why did He let this war happen? Why did He let my father be in prison? Why did He let that boy get killed who was about to get married? I don't see anything good about it."

"But, Jeff, you can't talk like that!"

Jeff's face was pale, even in the dawn light. "Leah, my mother died. I don't have any home anymore. My father's in prison. Maybe my brother's dead. What have I got to be happy about? Why should I trust God?"

He knew Leah had never heard him speak like this. He had always been a faithful attender at church.

She looked shaken. "Jeff," she whispered, "we've got to trust God." She moved to stand beside him. "We've got to remember things don't always go well, but God always does what is right. You know the Bible. Look at Daniel down in the lions' den. Why, things looked downright terrible for him! And the people of Israel, when they were caught and Pharaoh's army was about to kill them all. Think about them, what they must have felt—but Moses didn't doubt! He knew God was going to deliver them—in His own way. And He did."

"That was in the Bible," Jeff said. He turned and began skinning another fish. "But this is now, and somehow I just feel so—well, I don't know how to say it . . ."

Leah moved closer. She reached out and touched his arm. "Jeff, please don't talk like that! I know you feel bad, and I do too. But God wants us to trust Him. He's never failed anybody yet."

Jeff continued cleaning the fish, and Leah kept talking quietly, trying to encourage him.

Finally, when all the fish were cleaned, he said, "Let's go to the pump and wash these off."

She pumped while he washed the fish. When they turned to go to the house, he said, "I'll try to believe God will make things be right—but it sure is hard."

"I know." Leah's eyes were warm. "You and I, we're going to pray that your father will get out of jail—unless God has something better in mind. That would be something, wouldn't it?"

Jeff blinked, then nodded firmly. "That would be a miracle, and I guess I need a miracle these days." He looked at her and said, "Sorry to be such a crybaby. All of us need a miracle—you and your pa and mine, your whole family, all of us."

"We'll see it," Leah said confidently. "You wait and see!"

3
Rebel in Washington

Jeff looked out the sutler's wagon where he sat beside Leah and said sharply, "And this is the capital of the United States? I sure don't think much of it!"

Mr. Carter, appearing rather pale and worn after the difficult ride all the way from Kentucky to Washington, turned to the boy. "Well, this is the worst part of it—the city, son."

Leah had been pointing out the sights to Jeff all the way on the journey. Now she said, "This is what they call the Swampoodle District. It's not a good place, Jeff."

Jeff could not help thinking that Washington was the worst looking town he had ever seen. They were passing along the Old City Canal, which was nothing but a swamp filled with all kinds of garbage and smelling like a hog pen. Cattle and sheep and geese and dozens of dogs ran everywhere. The smell was overwhelming, and he grunted. "I guess I'll take Richmond anytime."

Leah's father grinned slightly. "Well, it don't smell too good," he admitted. "What's happened is, the country had ideas a mite too big. They wanted to build the capital as a symbol, so they spent a bunch of money putting up public buildings."

"Where are they?" Jeff demanded.

"Oh, they're spread out all over the place. There's the Capitol building and the Library of Congress and the Senate and the Hall of Representatives—but they're so scattered out you can't ever see them all together. Guess the government bit off more than it could chew."

"Don't look healthy to me." Jeff shook his head. "Looks like a swamp. I'll bet there's fever here."

"You're right about that," Leah put in. "Even the president's house is right in the middle of low ground, and everybody in town has malaria at one time or another—even the troops on the other side."

As the wagon rumbled over the cobblestone streets, Mr. Carter explained that they would have to pass through the center of town to get to the camp. Then he said, "Did you hear about the comet, Jeff?"

"Comet?" Jeff frowned. "No, what about it?"

"Oh, it come along last June, just before the big battle at Bull Run. It was something to see. The *New York Herald* wrote about it—said it was a celestial visitor that had sprung upon us."

"I remember that," Leah said. "It was just as clear as anything up there. It had a long tail, kind of a bright streamer, Jeff. Why, it seemed to light up the sky!"

"Lots of people thought it was come to warn us about something terrible, maybe from the Lord," her father said.

"Well, maybe it was," Jeff said. "The war came, didn't it?"

Mr. Carter nodded, then shouted at a flock of sheep that impeded the pathway of the horses. "Get out of there, you woollies!" he yelled, but the sheep, in the manner of such animals, took their time.

When they finally cleared the small flock, he muttered something about people who let their stock run loose. Then he said, "You know, I heard there was a slave woman, close friend of Mrs. Lincoln and the president. Way I heard it, she could conjure spells—course I don't believe in *that!* They said when she saw the comet she said, 'You see that great big fire sword blaze up in the sky? That mean there's a great war coming, and the handle's toward the North and the point's toward the South, and the North's gonna take that sword and cut the South's heart out. But that Lincoln man, if he takes the sword, he's gonna perish by it!'"

"I wonder if the president heard about that," Leah said.

"They say his son, Tad, heard the story and went to tell his father. Mrs. Lincoln scolded him, but the way I heard it the president seemed interested."

"Well, comet or no comet, there's a war," Jeff said grimly.

"And it won't last forever," Mr. Carter said. "Wars never do."

Leah reached over and squeezed Jeff's arm. When he looked at her, she nodded slightly. He guessed she was thinking of his promise not to give up but to trust God. It had been hard, but he smiled back and said no more about his doubts.

Two hours later they arrived at a large cluster of buildings. "What's this?" Jeff asked.

"This is what they call the Mall. There's the Patent Office over there, and the Post Office. What we're looking for is the War Department." Mr. Carter drove his team up to an imposing building and handed the lines to Leah. "You hold the horses. I'll see if we can find out about your pa, Jeff."

He clambered down from the wagon and moved slowly toward the building.

When he'd gone, Jeff said in a worried tone, "Your pa seems to be ailing. He's not well, is he?"

"No, he's not. Ma worries about him a lot. She didn't want him to come back on this trip."

Jeff turned and looked at her. "I think he came back just to help me. That's the idea I got." He bit his lip. "I hate to have him do that. I hate to ask favors."

Leah was wearing a light green dress that matched her eyes. She looked very pretty, he thought, even in such a plain outfit.

Now she put out her hand and touched his arm. "We're friends, aren't we? Friends do things for each other. Don't forget, we've asked God to get your father out, and we're going to trust Him to do what's best."

"I—I guess so. I'll try anyway."

They watched the traffic go by and the soldiers and the many civilians who bustled around to the different buildings. Finally Leah's father came back and climbed into the wagon.

"I couldn't get a permit for you to visit the prison, Jeff. The officer was gone who gives them out, but we'll try anyway."

He turned the wagon around, and they made their way through the city. Men in uniform were everywhere.

Leah had learned to recognize some of the uniforms from her work with her father. "Look! That's the Seventh New York. Aren't they smart?" She pointed out a group of soldiers in spick-and-span gray uniforms with pipe-clay cross belts on their breasts.

"Don't hardly see how they could fight in such fancy uniforms as that," Jeff mumbled. He took in the other troops that Leah and her father pointed out to him, men from Rhode Island, Massachusetts, Illinois, from all over the North.

At last they arrived at the camp itself, which seemed to Jeff to be an ocean of tents stretched out almost as far as he could see.

"We'll find our regiment and park the wagon. Maybe we'll have time to go in today, but I doubt it."

Mr. Carter threaded the wagon through the myriad tents and finally arrived at a section where he was greeted by an officer.

"Well, it's you, Dan! Glad to see you back again."

Pulling up the horses, Mr. Carter said, "Hello, Major Bates, good to see you. We've come back with a wagonload of supplies."

Major Bates was a tall man with a powerful voice. He commanded the Washington Blues. "The boys just got paid, so I expect they'll be coming to see you. I suppose you got lots of those tracts and Bibles to give away again?"

"Sure have, Major. Oh, this is a young friend of ours who's come with me and Leah to help with the work—Jeff Majors."

Major Bates nodded to Jeff. "Glad to have you." Then he turned and walked away.

"He's a pretty good officer but a little brash, they say," Mr. Carter remarked. "Well, let's get the wagon set up and the tent."

Thirty minutes later, Jeff, Leah, and her father had put up the large tent that would serve as sleeping quarters for the Carters. Jeff's own bunk was either under the wagon when the weather was nice or inside when it rained.

The sky was growing dark now, and Leah asked him to build a fire. When he had a good one going, she brought out the pots and pans, and soon the smell of cooking meat was in the air.

They sat down after a while and ate steak and beans. It all tasted wonderful to Jeff. Mr. Carter ate hardly anything, merely picking at his food.

They were almost finished when a voice called out, "Hey!" and Jeff looked up to see a short corporal in a blue uniform approaching them rapidly.

"Why, Ira, it's you!" Leah said.

She got up, putting her hand out, and the short soldier took it, grinning broadly. He had brown eyes and hair and seemed to Jeff to be more friendly than he should.

"Well, maybe I can get some letters written around here now—to that girlfriend of mine."

Leah laughed. "You forgot you told me you made up that girlfriend—Rosie—just to get me to write letters for you. What did you do with all those letters anyway?"

"Still got 'em." Ira grinned. He glanced over at Jeff and when he was introduced said, "Glad to have you, Jeff. Where you from?"

Jeff hesitated. He almost said that he came from Richmond, but he was saved when Mr. Carter said, "Why, he grew up just a whoop and a holler past our house. His family and ours have been close ever since these two were born."

"That so?" Ira Pickens nodded. "Well, that's good. Good to grow up knowing people. You two went to school together, I guess."

"Yes, and hunted wild birds' eggs, and went trot lining, and just about everything else."

"I guess we'll have plenty of time to get acquainted," Ira said. "After that licking we took back at Bull Run, looks like we ain't never going nowhere again."

Jeff filed that away for future reference and said nothing.

But Leah said, "Is the army pretty down and out, Ira?"

"Oh, I don't reckon so. We got us a new general—General McClellan. They call him 'Little Mac' behind his back. He's a whizzer though—knows how to make a fellow feel like a real winner! I guess we'll be ready to meet the Rebs pretty soon."

"Sit down and have some of this steak," Mr. Carter said.

The young soldier sat down and chatted amiably. After he had gone and Jeff was leaving to go to the wagon, he said, "He a pretty good friend of yours?"

"Yes, he is," Leah said. "He was wounded at Bull Run, and I helped take care of him. He's a nice young man. I hope nothing happens to him."

"Good night," Jeff said. "I'll see you in the morning."

He went to bed. The weather was hot, so he simply lay down on his blanket, listening to the sounds of the camp. Finally, he went to sleep, thinking, *I've got to see Pa—I've just got to!*

* * *

"I tell you, you can't see him. Not without a pass."

The speaker was a short, cocky lieutenant named Simpkins. He had scarcely been civil when Mr. Carter asked for permission to visit the Old

Capitol Prison, and now he shook his head vehemently. "I'm telling you, nobody's going into the prison without a pass from the War Department." He glared at the three who stood before him.

They had driven up to the Old Capitol Prison, which actually had been the capitol building of the country for a few days at one time. Then it had become a jail, a makeshift one. Little effort had been spent on it, Jeff saw, and it was in a dilapidated condition.

Simpkins shook his head. "No, sir, you'll have to go get a pass."

Jeff felt like arguing, but Mr. Carter said quickly, "All right, we'll do what we can, Lieutenant. Thank you."

When they were outside, Jeff burst out, "It wouldn't hurt him to let us in to see my pa."

"Jeff," Leah said quickly, looking around, "don't tell people that he's your pa. Just say it's a friend."

"That's right," her father said. "It would be harder to get a pass for a relative."

* * *

They didn't know that Lieutenant Simpkins had become totally suspicious of any visitors. His brother had been killed at Bull Run, and he hated all Southerners. Being in charge of the guard detail that ringed the Old Prison, he took it upon himself to turn away as many visitors as possible.

Turning now to the corporal who was standing at attention next to him, he said, "You see those three?"

"Yes, sir."

"If you see them again, tell me about it."

The corporal was a tall, thin, young man of eighteen, who had seen no action at all since being in the army. The thought of spies excited him. He said, "You think they could be spies?"

"Call me *sir*, corporal! *Sir!*" Simpkins gave the soldier a withering glance. "I'm not taking any chances. If they come around here again, you come and tell me about it at once."

"Yes, sir, I'll do that." When the lieutenant was gone, the tall, thin soldier stared at the three visitors as they departed. "Spies . . . well, I'll be . . . sure would like to catch me a couple or three spies!"

4
A Good Yankee

Leah found Jeff sitting under the shade of a towering oak staring moodily across the small meandering stream. For two days she had watched him grow more and more disappointed as no way was found to pay a visit to his father. Sitting down beside him on the log, she said, "Jeff, come along with Pa and me."

"Where you going?" he asked morosely.

"They're having a preaching service, and they say the preacher is really fine. He's one of the chaplains of the regiment."

Jeff picked up a stone, examined it for a moment, then threw it almost viciously in front of a squirrel that was scavenging along the ground. The squirrel jumped straight up and turned a back flip, which caused both of them to laugh. "Well, I guess that'll be all right," he said grudgingly, "but I don't put much stock in what any Yankee preacher would say."

He rose to his feet, and they wandered back to the wagon, where they found Leah's father putting on a clean white shirt.

"Always like to wear a clean shirt to go to meetin'." He smiled at them. "Come along now. We don't want to be late."

They made their way through the city of tents

and came at last to an open space already filled with blue uniforms.

"My, that's a big congregation," Leah said, staring over the crowd of soldiers. She looked up to where a small platform had been built. "That's him—Chaplain Marcus Patterson. They say he's bringing revival to the Union army."

Jeff saw a slight young man of perhaps thirty, wearing an officer's uniform. He had red hair and a small, trim mustache and beard.

"He's not as fat as some of the preachers we had back home, is he?"

"I don't guess he has the chance to sit down and eat fried chicken as much. They say he's on the go all the time," she replied. "I think the meeting's going to start."

A tall sergeant stood up then and, without saying a word, began to sing. He had a clear tenor voice, and soon the clearing was filled with the sound of more than a thousand male voices. They sang "The Old Rugged Cross," and Jeff thought of the hundreds of times he had sung that song in the little church back home.

Leah whispered to him when the song was over, "Someday we'll be back home singing this song again."

The song service went on for some time, for the men seemed to love to sing. Then the tall song leader stepped back, and the red-haired chaplain came forward. He had a clear, ringing baritone voice and could be heard distinctly back at the edge of the clearing where Jeff and Leah and Dan Carter stood.

"I'm not going to preach a long-winded sermon," he began, then smiled as some applause broke out. "You don't pay me enough for that, but I am glad to bring the gospel to you tonight." He looked over his congregation for a moment. Then he opened his Bible and read slowly, "'It is appointed unto man once to die, but after this the judgment.' That's half of my text. The second half is, 'For God so loved the world that he gave his only begotten Son that whosoever believeth in him should not perish but have everlasting life.'"

He began to preach, and Jeff found himself caught up in the sermon. The chaplain had the ability to weave stories in with Scripture—going to the Old Testament, then to the New, then illustrating from the lives of famous Christians. All men and women and young people must someday die, he said. If they die unprepared, they perish forever, cut off from God.

Then he came to the end of his sermon by stressing that Jesus paid it all. "You've heard a thousand times that Jesus died for our sins. But now that's more important for you men than ever before because the day of battle lies ahead." He looked out over the faces that peered up at him intently. "Some of you will not be here when I preach another sermon. Perhaps *I'll* not be here. I may be in the presence of God." He paused. "I'm going to give you the opportunity to know God. If you feel that you're a sinner and not right with Him, won't you come and let me pray with you?"

Jeff felt a stirring in his heart and knew that the sermon was for him. Stubbornly he planted his feet and stared at the ground. He was aware that many soldiers were walking forward. Men were falling on their knees at the platform, and when he glanced up he saw the chaplain praying with them.

But Jeff did nothing, and finally it was time to go.

Leah knew that Jeff was moved by the sermon, but she said nothing to him, knowing how he hated to be pushed. Later that night, just before she and her father retired, she said, "Pa, I think Jeff needs to find God. He's real bitter about his father."

"We'll pray for him, Pet. God will hear our prayers."

* * *

The next day, after selling supplies all morning long, Leah's father said, "Let's close up and go to the hospital. I want to talk to a few of the boys there."

Jeff accompanied them, having nothing else to do, and while they passed up and down the beds, he stood back, saying little. He was thinking, *These men are the enemy. They are the ones that shot my pa.*

But he watched Leah and her father move from bed to bed. They had already become acquainted with several of the wounded men. They stopped beside one bed where a boy of no more than eighteen lay. He had only one arm and had a bandage about his head. He listened as Leah talked to him. "Why, you'll be fine. You'll be going home now, Jesse," she said, "and your folks will be glad to see you."

Mr. Carter had moved on down to another bed, but Jeff stood watching Leah and the wounded soldier.

"Well," the boy said, "I don't know." He lifted his stub of an arm and said, "Don't reckon I'll be able to do much with this."

"Course you will," Leah said emphatically. "You'll just have to make that other arm stronger." She talked to him for a while and finally, when they moved on and were out of hearing, Jeff said, "That's pretty rough, having only one arm."

Leah sighed and looked back at the young man. "Yes, I feel so sorry for them all."

Jeff might have felt sorry himself, but he could not forget how hopeless it seemed to get in to see his father. He worried about his father a great deal, for he feared that his wound had not healed well.

They were almost ready to leave when all of a sudden Leah looked up and said, "Why, look, Jeff! There's the chaplain."

Chaplain Patterson was sitting beside the bed of a young man who had a bandage over his eyes.

Jeff said, "I guess he's a pretty hard-working fellow—for a preacher."

As they passed by, the chaplain rose, and Jeff heard him saying, "I'll be back to see you, Bobby. God's going to do a work in you, you'll see." He turned and almost bumped into Leah. He reached out to steady her and said, "Well, pardon me, miss, I didn't expect to see a young lady here."

Leah smiled at him. "My father's a sutler. My name is Leah Carter, and this is Jeff Majors. We enjoyed your sermon last night especially, chaplain."

"Did you now? Well, I'm glad to hear that." He stood there smiling, chatting, and soon he had found out all about the work that Leah and her father were doing. "Oh, yes, I've talked to several of the men who've gotten your Bibles and tracts—a wonderful work you and your father are doing. I'd like to meet him."

"He's right down there, Chaplain. Come along."

Leah led the chaplain to where her father was talking to a wounded soldier. After he had finished, she said, "Father, I want you to meet Chaplain Patterson."

The two men shook hands and chatted amiably. Patterson commended the sutler on the work he was doing. "Anything I can do to help you, you just let me know."

Dan Carter blinked in surprise as a sudden thought seemed to come to him. He glanced at Jeff. "Well, there is one thing. There's a friend of mine, an old neighbor from Kentucky. He joined the Southern army and was taken prisoner at Bull Run. He's in the Old Capitol Prison now."

Patterson shook his head, "Sad, isn't it, that things have to be like this?" Then he asked, "What can I do for you, Mr. Carter?"

"If you would help us get into the prison so that we could visit him, I'd appreciate it. He was wounded, and I don't think he's doing too well. I'd like to help him if I can."

"Why, of course. As a matter of fact, I visit there myself some. I'll pick up a pass for you and leave it with the officer in charge."

"Well—Lieutenant Simpkins, he's turned us down several times."

"Don't worry." The chaplain grinned. "I outrank him. You'll get in to see your friend. What's his name?"

"Lieutenant Nelson Majors. I appreciate this, Chaplain."

"Don't mention it. We must get together soon, and I'll be seeing you often because you'll be following the troops, I suppose?" When he received a nod from Carter, he said, "Well, we'll stay with these boys right up to the very cannon's mouth."

He turned and walked busily away.

Jeff said, "You think he'll do it?"

"Son," Dan said kindly, "I'm an old man, but I've learned to tell a truth teller from the other kind. Don't you worry. Chaplain Patterson will do exactly what he said."

Jeff was nervous all day. He had been impressed by the friendly chaplain but still couldn't quite believe it would happen.

Early the next morning he arose at dawn and walked over to the woods where he escaped the pressure of the crowds. For a long time he walked among the trees, following the little creek. Once a small bass broke the water, and he thought of Old Napoleon waiting in the pond back in Kentucky.

"I sure hope nobody catches you, Nap," he whispered. "That's one thing I want to do for myself."

When he got back to the camp, he found breakfast ready and sat down and ate the eggs and fried ham that Leah had prepared.

"Where did you get milk?" he said. "I don't see any cows around here."

"A woman came through selling it," Leah said. "Her husband was killed in one of the battles, so she makes her living selling milk to the soldiers now. I felt so sorry for her." She drank some milk herself. "It's hard to think how many widows there are, but maybe the war will be over soon."

After breakfast, they mounted the wagon and rode back into Washington.

As they got down at the Old Capitol Prison, Jeff's face was set.

"Don't worry, Jeff," Leah said confidently. "Chaplain Patterson will come through."

They entered and went to Lieutenant Simpkins's office where they found him sitting behind his desk. His face turned red. "It's *you* again!"

"Why, yes," Mr. Carter said pleasantly. "I understand that provisions have been made for us to visit Lieutenant Nelson Majors."

Simpkins jerked his drawer open, yanked out a paper, and stared at it. His mouth drew tight, and he nodded curtly. "Yes, this came this morning. You can go see your *friend*."

Jeff could see that the lieutenant was furious, but Mr. Carter said gently, "We appreciate your help, Lieutenant. We will try to be as little trouble as possible. Perhaps we can help with some of the things the men need, since that's what we do, you know."

"These are rebels," Simpkins snapped. "They deserve what they are getting! Corporal!" he called out. "Take these people to see Lieutenant Majors."

"Yes, sir!"

The guard led them down through a series of hallways. There was a run-down air about the place, and guards roamed the passages, holding muskets loosely.

"Nobody's ever escaped from Old Capitol," the guard said. "No, sir! And never will either. We've got orders to shoot if they even get close to a door or window."

Leah and Jeff glanced at each other, and Leah shook her head when Jeff was about to speak.

"Don't say anything," she whispered. "Come on."

They came to a door with a padlock. The guard unlocked it and swung the door back. "Just holler through the grill when you want to leave," he said rather cheerfully. "Somebody'll let you out." He stepped aside, and the three entered.

Jeff looked around. The room was small, approximately fifteen feet square, and seemed crowded. One window was open, bars crossing it, and it admitted enough light so that he could see the faces of the men. At first, he didn't see his father, and his heart sank. But then a voice came.

"Jeff!"

He turned quickly and saw a cot over in one corner, illuminated by the sunlight. His father was struggling to sit up. *"Pa!"* He helped his father into a sitting position. He was shocked at his father's face, for Lieutenant Majors had lost much weight. His eyes seemed sunken in his head, and his skin was sallow, unlike his usual ruddy tan.

"Pa!" he repeated. He put his arms around him and found, for once, that he was stronger than his father.

"Son!" the lieutenant said, holding to him hard for a moment. Then he pulled away, looked around at the other prisoners and said, almost in a whisper, "What are you doing here?"

Mr. Carter may have been afraid that Jeff might reveal more than he should. He came up and said, "Well, don't I get a 'hello,' Nelson?" He stepped into the light so that his face was revealed, and when the lieutenant called his name, he reached out and took his friend's hand.

"Me and Leah here and Jeff, we're doing sutler work now, you know. Heard you were in prison, so we thought we would come by for a visit." He glanced at Jeff and shook his head.

Nelson Majors seemed to get the message too. "Why, I'm glad to see you all," he said. "You fellows, let these visitors have some of those chairs. You can sit down anytime."

There was a murmur of assent, and some of the men at once brought chairs over. "Let me introduce you to some of these fellows," the lieutenant said. He called off their names, and when they had all been introduced, said, "Now, you tell me the news of home."

"We will," Leah said, "but first, we brought you something good." She had brought a large basketful of fresh bread and cakes and meat that she had prepared the night before, knowing they were coming. "I didn't know if they would let us bring this in or not, but they just looked through it and said there weren't any guns or knives here."

Jeff's father looked into the basket and shook his head in wonderment. "Manna from heaven! Here, you fellows—we're going to have a meal fit for a king. Then he added, looking at Leah with a smile, "From a princess."

Jeff never forgot the next few moments. The men were as starved as hungry wolves. They tried not to gobble the food, but he saw how hard it was for them.

Finally, after receiving their thanks over and over again, Leah said, "Jeff, you talk to the lieutenant. We've brought some Bibles and tracts for you all," she said to the other prisoners.

Jeff saw what she was doing. In the crowded room she was going to draw them off, talk to them, ask their names, keep their attention away from Jeff and his father.

"Guess I better lie down, Son. Can't sit up too long." Lieutenant Majors stretched out painfully, then looked around and whispered, "Son, you've got to get out of here."

Jeff leaned forward, his face a few inches from his father's, and also whispered, "I had to come, Pa. I knew you were sick, and I had to come and see if I could help."

"That's like you, Son, but if they found out I was your father, you'd be suspected at once."

"Suspected of what?"

"Of being a spy." Nelson Majors shrugged his thin shoulders. "They think everybody's a spy these days. There are a lot of spies in Washington. And I guess there's some Union spies in Richmond." He looked up. "Well, now that you're here, tell me everything. How have you been? How's Tom? How's Esther?"

Jeff sat there for thirty minutes telling his father about what he had been doing. His heart was heavy when he saw the dullness of his father's eyes and remembered how bright-eyed and strong and cheerful he'd always been. *Being a prisoner is killing him*, he thought. *He's got to get out of this place.*

Lieutenant Majors listened quietly. Then he said, "Son, you've done all you can. Now I want you to leave. You've got to get back to Virginia. Get back with Tom—you two take care of each other as best you can."

"But what about you?"

"God will take care of me. He sent you by, didn't he? And Dan and Leah? You've got to take care of yourself."

"You think you'll ever get exchanged, Pa?"

"Well, that's not going too well, but there's always hope." He reached up a thin hand and took Jeff's. "I want you to know I'm proud of you, Jeff. You're a man already, despite your years."

Jeff flushed and shook his head. "Aw, I haven't done anything. There must be some way to escape from this place."

"*No!* Don't even think of that!" his father exclaimed. "I want you to promise me you won't try anything foolish like trying to get me out of here. You promise that, Jeff?"

Jeff nodded, saying, "Yes, sure, I promise, Pa—but you've got to get out of here somehow."

"We'll talk about it. You'll be here for a while, won't you? With the Carters?"

"Yes, they say the army's building up. General McClellan wants a hundred thousand men—that's what everybody says. So we'll stay until they leave."

"Good. It means a lot to have you here, Son."

The three stayed for some time, and when they left Jeff saw Lieutenant Simpkins glaring as they passed his doorway. As they got into the wagon, Jeff said, "Lieutenant Simpkins doesn't trust us. He thinks everybody's a spy."

"You'll have to be very careful," Mr. Carter warned. "Don't say anything to give yourself away. I'd hate to see you taken and put in prison."

They sat quietly on the wagon seat as they rode away, each filled with his own thoughts. After a while Leah said, "We'll come back every day, Jeff. We'll bring medicine, and we'll get Chaplain Patterson to help, and your father will get better—you'll see!"

5

Letter from Richmond

Jeff went every day to visit his father. Usually Leah and Mr. Carter went with him, but sometimes he went alone. He was glad to see that the food seemed to help, and Mr. Carter also took along some of his medicine to share with the lieutenant.

Jeff was thinking about this one day during breakfast when Leah said, "We're going to church this morning."

"Going to church? Is the chaplain having another meeting for the men?"

"Oh, no. This is a big church downtown. We've heard about the preacher there, and Pa wants to go hear him."

"I don't think I want to go hear any more sermons," Jeff muttered.

But in the end Leah had her way. She disappeared into her tent and came out wearing a pink dress that he'd always thought was pretty, with a bonnet to match and a pair of light brown kid boots. "Now, you go get yourself ready," she said, "and be sure you comb your hair. It looks like a rat's nest!"

Jeff did as he was told, and later, when the three of them filed into the big church in downtown Washington, he was impressed with the ornate building. As they took a seat halfway down, he whispered to Leah, "This sure doesn't look like our little church back home. I'll bet the preaching isn't as good either."

Leah started to answer. Then she glanced backward and caught her breath. "Look!" she whispered.

Jeff turned to look, and he, too, blinked in surprise. "Is that President Lincoln?"

"Yes—and that's his wife and their son with him."

Jeff had seen pictures of the president drawn by artists for the Southern newspapers. They always portrayed him as a hideous creature. They called him "The Gorilla." Jeff fixed his eyes on Lincoln's face and thought, *Why, he's not ugly at all. Homely, maybe—but not like a gorilla.*

As the president approached, he studied him. Abraham Lincoln did have a homely face. He had deep-set eyes and sunken cheeks, a pouting lower lip, and a wart. *But he's not ugly, and he doesn't look like a murderer, which they all call him,* Jeff thought.

He watched the president lead his wife and son to a seat across from him and slightly in front. When they sat down, he whispered to Leah, "He doesn't look like I thought he would."

All during the sermon Jeff kept glancing at the president. He could see his profile and noted that the president was listening carefully. Once he turned to look around, and he met Jeff's eyes. Jeff flushed, but President Lincoln just smiled and nodded slightly, then turned back toward the platform.

On their way home, Jeff said, "You know, Lincoln's not like I thought he would be."

"How's that, Jeff?" Mr. Carter asked.

"Well, you know—in the Southern newspapers they make him out to be some kind of a . . . a monster, a murderer. They say he started the war."

52

"That's not right," Mr. Carter said gently. "This war was the last thing Abraham Lincoln wanted. All he wants now is to keep the Union together."

"He wants to set all the slaves free," Jeff corrected.

"Jeff, he said once in a speech that if he could save the Union by freeing some of the slaves and not freeing others, he'd do it. If he could save it by freeing all the slaves, he'd do that. But if he could save it by freeing none of the slaves, he'd do that. But he means to save this Union of ours."

Jeff thought about President Lincoln a great deal for the next few days. Seeing him had shaken his ideas about the war itself. As long as he'd thought of Lincoln as an evil man who wanted to wreck the South out of pure meanness, it was easy to think about fighting. But Lincoln's face was kind. Just one look and Jeff had known that he was not evil. So he kept quiet, just once in a while mentioning the president to Leah.

A few days after the service, Dan Carter came to Jeff with an envelope. "Letter for you, Jeff. It came addressed to me. It went to our home in Kentucky first, and my wife mailed it on."

Jeff took the piece of paper, opened it, and recognized the handwriting at once. "Why, it's from Tom." He scanned the brief page and looked up with a worried expression. "Tom says I've got to come back. If I don't, I'll be posted as a deserter."

"Oh, Jeff! Then you'll have to go," Leah said.

"Yes, I'm afraid you will, my boy. You wouldn't want to be a deserter."

Jeff glanced quickly at the older man and saw that he was being honest. He thought again, *Yankees can't be all that they told us they were. But I guess people have told them the same kind of stuff about us.* Aloud he said, "I'll have to go tell Pa."

"Go by yourself this time. Take the horse," Mr. Carter said. "I'll find out about the trains and see about tickets."

Jeff left at once. He tied the horse outside the Old Capitol Prison, was admitted, and once again passed under the hard eyes of Lieutenant Simpkins. "Well, at least I won't have to see him anymore," he muttered to himself.

In the prison cell he found his father shaving.

"Sit down, Jeff, while I scrape these whiskers off." Lieutenant Majors drew the blade carefully down his cheek, wiped the lather onto a towel, and then took another pass at his face. "What's been going on?"

Jeff hesitated, then he told his father about President Lincoln and how he felt about him and how it had disturbed him.

Nelson Majors finished the shave, listening carefully. Then he put the razor away. "Well, Yankees are just people like we are. We can't hate them, Jeff. We believe differently, but we're one people."

"I guess I'll have to change the way I think a little bit, Pa." He knew he had to tell his father something else. "I got a letter from Tom. He said I'd have to go back or be posted as a deserter."

At once Nelson Majors said, "I've been half expecting that, and you'll have to go, of course."

"Yes, that's what Mr. Carter says, but I hate to leave you, Pa."

They talked for a long while, knowing it would be the last time. When Jeff got up to go, he cried out, "Pa, it's awful! I just can't go and leave you alone like this!"

54

"Son," the lieutenant said, putting his arm around Jeff's shoulder, "you're almost a man now, and one of the things you learn as a man is that you can't always control circumstances—bad things do happen. Nothing you can do about it." He looked at Jeff carefully, his handsome face very sober. "But a man can always control how he acts in the circumstances. So that's what we'll have to do. For now, it's your job to go back to be a soldier. It's my job to stay here until the Lord sees fit to release me. We'll just have to do our job, even though it's hard. All right?"

"Sure, Pa. It's just—not easy."

"Hard things are what make a man better. Not easy things. It's hard for me too—but you can write to me, and we'll both believe the Lord to bring us through it all."

Jeff did not stay longer. He still could not bear the thought of leaving his father.

When he got back to camp, Dan Carter must have seen the boy was upset, but he merely said, "The train leaves at three o'clock. We'll take you— me and Leah."

"Yes, sir. And I want to thank you for all you've done for my father and for me. I don't know how we would have made it without the Carters."

"We're neighbors, aren't we? You'd do the same for us."

* * *

That afternoon when it was time to go, Jeff was out by the creek when Leah found him. She knew it was the one place he could find quiet, and they'd walked along this stream many times, watching the minnows and frogs.

He was standing beside the bank, looking down into the water, as she came up beside him. "Almost time to go, Jeff."

Jeff looked at her, then put his boot in the stream and watched the water curl over his toe, making a miniature waterfall. "Just like the creek back home, isn't it, Leah? Do you ever think of those times we fished there?"

"Yes, I think about that a lot."

"I wish we could go back! I wish we could go back to what we were. Remember? I'd like to be hunting birds' nests, and running a trot line, and going coon hunting—doing all the things we used to do. Those were the best days of my life."

Leah felt so sorry for him she wanted to cry. She felt sorry for herself too. She made herself say, as cheerfully as possible, "I guess it's like this creek. The water passes us, it goes somewhere else—it can't go back."

"My grandpa," Jeff said, "always told me you couldn't step in the same river twice. I guess that's what that means—the river goes, and it's gone. Just like us."

"Oh, not quite like that, Jeff. The river can't remember, but we can. We can remember those days, and somehow that means they're not altogether gone if we can remember them together."

Jeff turned and admired the sheen of her blonde hair as the sun struck it. "You're growing up fast," he said, "and getting to be a wise woman too. Sound like a philosopher."

"Oh, you know I'm not that, Jeff."

"Well, all I can say is that I'm getting tired of saying good-bye to folks. I wish we didn't have to, but we do."

Leah took his hand, then hesitated. "Come on, let's go to the train, and we'll write each other often. Remember, say something real, real sweet to me, will you, Jeff?"

Jeff stared at her, his cheeks flushing. "I can't do that!"

"Yes, you can. It'll be in code, so nobody will know it."

"I don't know how to write in code!"

"It's easy," Leah said, her eyes glowing. "I read about it in a novel. What we'll do is this—we'll write with lots of space between the lines. Then we'll write with a special ink in the spaces. Then when we put the letters in the oven or over a fire, they'll turn brown!"

"We don't have any magic ink like that," Jeff protested.

"We can use lemon juice. I've already tried it, and it works real good. It's invisible until you heat it up."

"Well, it might be a good idea," Jeff said slowly. "There'll be some things I wouldn't want anybody to read. But what do you mean about writing sweet things?"

"You know, tell me something about me that you like real well."

Jeff laughed aloud. "You are a vain little thing, aren't you? All right, I'll do that. I promise."

Standing at the train, Jeff shook Mr. Carter's hand. Then he awkwardly shook hands with Leah. "I'll do what I said," he promised her. "Good-bye."

He boarded the train, and soon it was out of sight.

"Hard to give him up, isn't it, Pet?" her father said.

"Yes, it is. I'm going to be so lonely." She looked up at him, and tears glittered in her eyes. "I wish we never had to say good-bye to anybody."

"So do I, Pet. So do I!"

6

General Lee Gets Whipped

On returning to Richmond Jeff soon found that things had changed greatly. The excitement after the victory at Bull Run was still there to a degree, but the casualties of the battle were horrible. The Federals had 1,500 dead and wounded and had lost more than 1,400 as prisoners. These, Jeff learned, had been herded through Richmond, where crowds chanted, "Live Yankees! Live Yankees!"

"How many did our side lose in all, Tom?" Jeff asked. The two of them were trudging along a dusty road in a column of Richmond Blues.

It was late September now. The August heat was gone, while just over the horizon there was a hint of cold weather even this early.

Tom glanced at his younger brother. The dust coated his dark face but did not disguise his good looks. "Well," he said thoughtfully, "we lost about two thousand killed, wounded, and captured."

Jeff looked up, startled, "Two thousand of our men? That's awful!"

"Yes, it is," Tom agreed glumly. "We captured about six thousand small arms and fifty-four cannon, and lots of rounds of ammunition, but that doesn't make up for the fellows we lost."

"I don't see why we didn't go on in when we won the battle and take Washington," Jeff grumbled. He shifted his drum to a more comfortable position and looked down the long line of marching men. "Everybody says we could have done it—even Stonewall said so."

Tom shook his head. "I kind of doubt it. We were just about as worn out as they were. If we'd gotten to Washington, they'd have had lots of fresh troops. The thing that worries me is that we don't seem to be taking this war seriously."

"What do you mean?"

"Why, from what I hear, the North is gearing up to make all kinds of guns, muskets, and cannons —but we don't seem to realize that we're going to be coming up against that sort of thing. Matter of fact, from what I hear, all our leaders are doing is just quarreling with each other. Jeff Davis seems to be catching a lot of it. Not easy to be a president, I guess."

A flight of blackbirds flew over, making their raucous cries. Jeff watched, then put his mind back to the journey in front of them. "Where's this place we're going to, Tom?"

"A place called Cheat Mountain. The Federals have taken a pass there, and General Lee says we've got to get them out."

The column marched on until the sun grew low over the hills. Then the troops broke out their gear for preparing supper, and soon the smell of cooking meat tantalized Jeff's nostrils.

He and five others had banded together to form a little group. One of them carried a pot, which the other squads seemed anxious to borrow.

Charlie Bowers, at the age of thirteen, was probably the youngest drummer in the Confederate

Army. He and Jeff wolfed down their portions, sitting off to one side. Charlie looked at his empty plate and shook his head. "I don't ever get enough to eat."

Jeff grinned at the smaller boy. "I don't see where you put it all. The food you eat is bigger than you are."

Curly Henson, a huge red-haired man, was sitting across the fire from Jeff. He had been a bully when Jeff first joined up, but the two had become fast friends when Henson saved his life. Now he said, "You two tadpoles need to be back home. This war is a job for men."

Jeff picked up a stone and tossed it over at him. "You watch your mouth, Curly," he said. "You won't be able to keep up with me on this march, hauling all that excess weight you got."

Laughter went around the campfire, and Sergeant Henry Mapes, a tall, rangy man with black hair and eyes, said, "You better save some of that for the fight that's coming up."

"Why, we'll push them Yankees right out of their holes," Curly said confidently. "We showed 'em at Bull Run, didn't we?"

"Yeah! And this time we got General Lee commanding," Jeff said.

He had unlimited confidence in Lee, as had most of the men. Lee received his full general's commission a few months ago and was leading the attack.

Suddenly Sergeant Mapes said, "Look at that!"

They all turned to look at a large man on horseback who had ridden by them, headed for the commander's tent. As he dismounted; Sergeant Mapes said, "That's Rooney Lee, General Lee's second son."

"He's a big'un, ain't he?" Jed Hawkins was a small, lean man with black hair. He had brought along his guitar—which was strictly against orders. He was plucking the strings lightly now. "I don't see how he gets a horse big enough to carry him."

Mapes frowned. "One of the problems about this whole campaign is there's too many chiefs and not enough Indians."

"What do you mean by that?" Jeff inquired.

"I mean we got four commanding officers, and that's too many." He named them, holding up one finger at a time. "We got General Loring, who's supposed to be sort of head of the whole thing. Then we got General Henry Wise, who used to be governor of Virginia. And we got John B. Floyd— he's an ex-governor too. Then, of course, we got General Lee."

Jed Hawkins laughed. "There's enough generals to fight all by themselves. We ought to go back to Richmond." He began plunking a tune on his guitar and soon raised his fine tenor voice in a rollicking song.

> "Oh, I'm a good old rebel,
>   Now that's just what I am,
> For this 'Fair Land of Freedom'
>   I do not care at all.
> I'm glad I fit against it,
>   I only wish we'd won;
> And I don't want no pardon
>   For anything I've done.

"I hates the Constitution,
    This Great Republic too,
I hates the Freedman's Bureau
    In uniforms of blue;
I hates the nasty eagle,
    With all his brags and fuss,
The lyin', thievin' Yankees,
    I hates 'em wuss and wuss.

"I hates the Yankee nation,
    And everything they do,
I hates the Declaration
    Of Independence too;
I hates the glorious Union—
    'Tis dripping with our blood—
I hates their striped banner—
    I fit it all I could."

After the last word of the song died down, Tom came by and sat beside Jeff. The others were carrying on a card game very noisily across the fire. "Tell me again about Pa," he said.

Jeff had told Tom several times about his visits to his father. He shook his head, saying, "I can't tell you any more, Tom. Just that he doesn't look good. Of course, he's a lot better since Mr. Carter and Leah started taking that good food in. I think he might have died if he hadn't gotten a little nourishment."

Tom stared into the fire silently, occupied with his thoughts. Finally he picked up a stick and stuck the end of it in the fire until it burst into flame and held it up as he would a candle. The darkness was falling, and his face was tense. "I hate everything about it," he said, "but I guess there's nothing we can do."

"Well, at least we're sure he'll be fed." Jeff took another bite of one of the biscuits he'd brought with him and chewed it thoughtfully. "As long as the Carters are there, they'll see that he gets good food and warm blankets and whatever else that will make life better."

"I got a letter from Sarah," Tom said abruptly. His face brightened. "I sure do miss that girl. She's the prettiest thing I've ever seen." Then he grew gloomy. "But she says she'll never marry me—not with things like they are."

"Things are kind of upside down. Someday, though, they'll be all right—at least that's what we're praying for, me and Leah."

Tom looked at his younger brother with a warm expression on his face. "I'm glad to hear that. It's going to take prayer to get this thing seen to."

The two sat for a long time, then finally rolled up in their blankets. Jeff lay awake listening to an owl calling from somewhere far away. It made a plaintive sound. He remembered what he had promised Leah and, just before he went to sleep, he prayed for his father and for Tom and for Royal and for all the family.

* * *

The battle of Cheat Mountain was a disaster from the very beginning. The Confederate force had lost many of its fighting men with measles and typhoid fever. The North Carolina Sixteenth Regiment had two-thirds of its men down, and Jackson's Brigade was not much better.

64

On the third morning of their march, Jeff had just pulled his drum over his shoulder as the men were falling in, when he heard Charlie Bowers say, "Look! There comes General Lee!"

The general was walking along, leading his horse, stopping to talk to soldiers here and there.

"Ain't he the finest-looking man you ever saw?" Charlie said warmly, "And the best soldier too. Lincoln tried to get him to be commander of the whole army of the North, but he wouldn't do it."

Jeff watched avidly as General Lee approached and was somewhat taken aback when he stopped directly in front of their squad.

"Good morning, men," he said. He had a bluff, reddish face and didn't look as tall as he did when he was mounted on his horse. Tom had told him, "He's got short legs, but he's tall from the waist up."

Now Jeff nodded and muttered with the rest of them, "Good morning, General."

Lee studied the faces of the two younger boys. "How old are you two soldiers?"

"I'm thirteen, General Lee, going on fourteen," Charlie Bowers said.

Jeff said, almost as if in an echo, "I'm almost fifteen, General."

Lee smiled and nodded his head. "We're glad to have two fine young men like you to help us in our campaign. I trust you'll come through the battle safely." He looked down the line at the other soldiers, who were listening eagerly, and said, "We must do our best, men. The South is depending on us."

"We will, General—don't you worry, General Lee. We'll whip 'em."

Cries went out up and down the line, and Lee took off his hat and waved it, saying, "I know you'll do your best." Then he turned and led his horse along, talking to other men down the line.

"I feel like we can't lose with a man like that. Don't you, Jeff?" Charlie said.

"Sure do! He's something, isn't he!"

The meeting with General Lee was the high point of the campaign as far as Jeff was concerned. He never forgot it.

And then it began to rain. One time Jeff saw a mule slide twenty feet down a wet, slippery slope, and the soldiers exhausted themselves trying to get it back up the mountainside.

"I never saw as much rain as this," Tom complained. "Rains every day. Every time you yell 'hello' you get a shower. Then some of the men had to shoot their guns to get the loads out. That brought on a regular flood."

Somehow they made their way forward but ran into such bad terrain that the cannon had to be abandoned. They spent their nights in the cold mountains. The rain spoiled their rations, the muskets were wet, and the gunpowder was ruined. The troops were forbidden to light fires.

Jeff wrote a letter to his father. "We tried to sleep—but the rain poured so and the torrents ran down the mountains with such a flood of water, we'd have been drowned if we'd laid down on the ground."

Finally, however, General Lee got his forces into position. He sent out scouts, among them his son, Rooney, and a colonel named Washington. The colonel was killed, and Rooney and his riders barely escaped.

Yet it was not the rain that cost the South the battle, but the behavior of a man called Colonel Rust. When he captured some Federal pickets, they told him such tales of Federal strength that he simply gave up.

On the night of October 6, the Confederates heard wheels rumbling and thought that the enemy was about to attack. Jeff and Tom stood close together, drenched through, and Jeff said, "I guess they're coming, don't you reckon?"

"I don't see how they could attack in a rain like this. Not one musket in ten would go off with the powder wet," Tom answered.

When at last daylight came, Lee discovered that the Federals were gone. The Cheat Mountain campaign was over. Lee stayed on for a few days, but the weather was now so bitter that there was little to do.

On the way back to Richmond the men grumbled, but when they got there they discovered that the story of the so-called battle had preceded them, and it was General Lee who took the criticism. Newspapers were calling him "Granny Lee," saying he didn't have what it took to be a general.

But Jeff learned what a real leader was like, for when General Lee addressed the troops, he showed no sign of disappointment. He encouraged them by telling them they had done their best. "You men proved yourselves as soldiers," he said. "I'm proud of you, for you did all that men could do, and we will fight again."

Later, as Jeff and Tom took up their quarters in Richmond, Jeff said, "Well, that wasn't much of a fight, was it? I feel sorry for General Lee."

Tom shook his head, "He didn't have a chance. All those other generals messed it up. But you'll see—we haven't heard the last of General Robert E. Lee."

7

A Beautiful Spy

My, it's cold out here, Pa!" Leah drew her wool coat closer around her and looked up at the sky. "It's going to snow again tonight, I believe."

It was the first day of January 1862, and the weather had already been harsh. The sound of the horses' hooves was muffled by the snow underfoot as Mr. Carter drove them quickly.

Her father agreed. "Well, starting out a new year with snow is as good a way as any."

They arrived at the prison, and he tied the horse to the rail. "We'll have to make two trips this time, Leah."

"No, we can take it all, Pa. Here, pile it up high on my arms."

He grinned with stiff lips. "All right, let's see if we can." The two of them stacked the packages of food and clothing and blankets they had brought and were admitted almost at once.

The guard spoke to them like an old friend. "Looks like you brought those Rebs lots of good stuff this time. How 'bout us poor Yankees?"

Leah smiled at him. "I did bring you a cake, believe it or not, Tommy. Let me get it." She fished in one of the sacks, pulled out a smaller package wrapped in brown paper, and handed it to him with a smile. "There, don't say I never gave you anything."

The guard whipped open the package and took a huge mouthful from the wedge of gingerbread that was inside. "Hoo-eee, this is good. Thanks a lot, Miss Leah, and you too, Mr. Carter. Go right on in. Those fellows will be glad to see you."

The guard was not wrong, for when the two with all their gifts were admitted into the small room, the prisoners crowded around them.

"Looks like Christmas isn't over yet," Jeff's father said. He had risen to greet them and take the thick, blue sweater that Leah handed him. "This ought to keep me warm enough, all right." He grinned.

"We tried to get something for each of you," her father said, handing out garments to the soldiers. "Nothing will fit, I suppose."

"Aw, that don't matter, Mr. Carter. We sure appreciate it, Miss Leah." A tall, redheaded soldier was buttoning up a wool coat that was at least two sizes too small. He hugged it to himself. "This will shore help on these cold nights."

The soldiers had learned to look forward to the visits of Daniel and Leah. It brightened their gloomy existence, for the Capitol Prison was a dismal place. Lice and bedbugs abounded, and spider webs decorated the soiled whitewash of the walls. The usual food was rank-tasting pork and beef, half-boiled beans, and musty rice. Over all was the stench of the open toilet situated behind the cookhouse in the yard.

After speaking with the men a while, Leah said, "I'm going to take some of this food down to Sergeant Chaffee."

She had made a friend of one of the men in another room and left to find him. As she was walking down the hall, she met an unusual sight—a tall woman, whose smoothly parted hair was threaded with gray, was being ushered along by a civilian. She held the hand of a young girl no more than seven or eight, whose eyes were frightened.

Leah stepped back to let them pass, and the little girl watched her carefully. When they were gone, Leah continued on down to give the food to the sergeant and his friends. Later, when she and her father were leaving, they stopped to talk to the guard who had eaten the gingerbread.

"Did you see Mrs. Greenhow?" he asked, his eyes bright with excitement.

"I saw a lady and a little girl," Leah answered.

"Well, you know who she was, don't you?" Tommy demanded. "That's Mrs. Greenhow, the famous Rebel spy!"

Dan Carter looked up, interest on his face. "So that's Mrs. Greenhow! I've heard quite a bit about her."

"Who is she, Pa?"

"She was a very prominent social lady in Washington. She married a doctor. She's a widow now."

"What's she doing in jail? This is no place for a woman," Leah said.

"You didn't hear about that, Miss Leah?" the guard asked. "She was the one that made the South win the Battle of Bull Run."

Leah stared at him. "How could that be?"

"Why, she found out the North's plans, and she got the news back to President Davis. That's how the South knew exactly what we were going to do. Oh, she's a smart one all right. No telling how much damage she done us."

Dan shook his head sadly. "I hate to see a woman in a place like this, though. What about the little girl?"

"I hear she's going to stay with her."

"Oh! That's awful!" Leah said. "A little girl like that in a place like this!"

The guard looked a bit embarrassed. "Yes, I guess it is, Miss Leah. But Mrs. Greenhow, she wouldn't have it no other way."

Leah and her father spoke for a while to the guard, but he knew little else about the woman. Later they found out that the head of the Federal Secret Service, Allen Pinkerton, had captured Mrs. Greenhow personally.

Leah said little, but when she talked about it later before bed, she said, "You know, I'm going to try to get to see Mrs. Greenhow and especially that little girl. She's bound to be scared, don't you think, Pa?"

"I wouldn't be surprised. That would be a good thing to do."

The next day Leah found a doll in one of the shops in Washington. It was not a new doll, but she bought it and wrapped it up in a piece of red paper. When she got to the prison, she asked for permission to see the little girl.

Lieutenant Simpkins glared at her as usual. "What do you want to see her for? So you can carry messages out to help the Rebels again?"

Leah was accustomed to his surly manner. "No, Lieutenant. You can search me all you want to. I just feel sorry for her little girl. I brought her a doll."

"Let me see that!" Simpkins looked at the doll, felt its soft body for messages, then handed it back. "Well, I guess it'll be all right. *This* time."

"Thank you, Lieutenant."

Mrs. Greenhow, she discovered, was on the second floor, and Leah was admitted at once. As soon as she was inside she said, "Mrs. Greenhow, my name is Leah Carter. My father is a sutler, but we visit the prisoners here."

"Are you a Southern sympathizer?" the woman asked. She was an attractive woman, but there was suspicion in her eyes. "Why would you visit Rebel prisoners?"

Leah explained that one of the prisoners had been a neighbor back in Kentucky, and then she smiled. "I thought you wouldn't mind if I would come and visit with your daughter. I brought her a present."

"A present?" Mrs. Greenhow's eyes softened. She turned to look at her daughter. "Isn't that nice, Rose?"

The child had held back. Now she reached out and took the parcel that Leah offered her. She opened it silently, but when she saw the doll, she cried, "Oh, Mama! It's just like the one I used to have back home!" She hugged the doll and looked at Leah. "Thank you."

"I had a doll like that too, when I was your age," Leah said. "Look—I brought some material too. Maybe we can make some clothes for her."

Leah sat down and for the next hour occupied herself with making doll clothes.

Mrs. Greenhow sat at a table watching. When Leah got up to leave, she put her hand out. "I'm poor in everything except thanks, Leah," she said. "I appreciate your coming. Will you come back again?"

"Oh, yes, my father and I come several times a week. Can I bring you anything, Mrs. Greenhow?"

Mrs. Greenhow looked at her carefully, then said, "The only thing would be some paper and something to write with."

"Oh, yes, we sell those to the soldiers all the time," Leah said. "As a matter of fact, I have some left over here." She rummaged in her bag and brought out a small package of paper, a pen, and a bottle of ink.

"I can't pay you for these."

"Oh, that's all right," Leah said quickly with a smile. "Just think of it as a late Christmas present." She put her things together, then left.

When she made her visit to Lieutenant Majors, Leah found that everyone was very interested in the woman.

"I'm surprised that Lieutenant Simpkins let you see her," Jeff's father remarked.

"Well, he did search the doll I took to her little girl." Leah grinned. "I think he was ashamed to. I think they're all ashamed of keeping a woman in a prison like this."

One of the prisoners who had been sitting close enough to overhear said, "Some talk about hanging her."

"Oh, they wouldn't do that!" Leah cried out.

"No, I don't think they would. That would be too terrible," Nelson Majors agreed. He looked at Leah and said, "You better be a little bit careful though. They're going to be watching everyone that comes to see Mrs. Greenhow. She's a famous person."

His warning alerted Leah, but during the next week she came to the prison several times, each time stopping by to see the woman and the little girl.

Every time, Lieutenant Simpkins searched her bags before she went in and as she left. Once he said, "I don't understand you. That woman's an enemy of your country."

Leah thought he was a sad looking young man, rather sour and bitter. "I don't know about that," she said. "I do know she's not young anymore, and I don't think little Rose is an enemy to anybody's country."

"That's what you think!" Simpkins said. "I tried to be nice to her the other day, and you know what that child said?" A look of disgust crossed his face. "She said, 'You've got one of the blamedest little Rebels here you ever saw.'" Simpkins shook his head in disgust. "What can you expect though with a mother like that?"

Leah did not argue with the lieutenant but made her way back to camp. When she got there she was met by her father.

"Come in and get warm, Pet."

She removed her heavy coat and hugged the little cookstove he had set up in the tent.

"How was Mrs. Greenhow and little Rose?"

"Oh, about as usual. So sad their being there! I wish they could leave."

"Well, I expect they'll be released and sent South one of these days," he said. "How about Nelson?"

"He looked fairly well," Leah said, holding out her hands to warm the numb fingers.

"Well, I've got something for you."

He held out an envelope, and when Leah saw the handwriting, she cried out, "It's from Jeff!"

She ripped it open and stared at the single sheet of paper. When she had read it, she then read it aloud to her father.

Dear Leah and Mr. Carter,

I find myself well and hope that you are the same. I trust that things have been going well with my father. I can't tell you how much Tom and I appreciate what you've done for him. I really don't think he would have made it if you hadn't been there.

We haven't done much soldiering here during the winter. It's too cold, I suppose. I think a lot about Esther. Tom and I both would like to see her. I want to get back to Kentucky as quick as I can. Of course, Tom wants to go too, but I think you know someone he wants to see just as much as he wants to see Esther.

Thanks for the long letters you've written me. I look forward to them. I think a lot about the birds' nest collection and wonder if we'll ever get one of those downy woodpecker eggs. Remember how hard we looked for that one last summer? And how you fell out of the tree, right on top of me? I didn't know you were so heavy until you lit right on top of my head.

Well, that's about all I have time for now. I will write again when I get your letter.

Yours sincerely,
Jefferson Majors

"A nice letter," Dan Carter said. "You can tell the boy's lonesome—but that's only natural."

Leah looked at him with a light in her eyes. "That's not all the letter," she said mysteriously.

"It's not? Is there more on the other side?"

"No, but we've got a secret code. Look here, Pa."

Leah held the paper near the flame that burned in the small stove.

"Why, you're going to burn it up, Daughter!" her father protested.

But she only shook her head. Carefully she held the letter close to the heat until it grew warm to the touch. She bent over, peering at it, then cried, "That's it!"

"That's what?" he asked in bewilderment.

"Look, Pa!" Leah held up the letter, and he pulled out his spectacles. Putting them on his nose, he leaned forward. "Why, what's that between the lines?"

"That's our secret code. It's written in lemon juice, and when you heat it, it comes out all nice and brown. See?"

"Well, I never heard the like of that! What does it say?"

Leah had to peer closely to read the secret writing.

> Leah, me and Tom will be leaving soon. We're going to some place called Fort Donelson in Tennessee. Word is here that some Yankee general, somebody called Grant, is going to try to take it, and we're going to have to stop him. Don't tell anybody about this. I guess we'll be in fighting, so if you want to pray for me and Tom, it'll be all right. We're still the best of friends.

Leah looked up and whispered, "We can't tell anybody about this, Pa, or we'd be spies."

"No, and I guess you better burn that letter."

"No, I won't do that, but I'll hide it so nobody will ever find it." Leah clutched the letter tightly and whispered, "Fort Donelson—I don't even know where that is."

"Well, I do. It's on a river in Tennessee, and it's not good for us."

"Why not, Pa?"

"Because, Pet, that's where your brother, Royal, has been sent, him and some of the troops to reinforce General Grant."

Leah looked startled. "Oh, that's awful! Why, that could mean that Royal and Tom could be shooting at each other."

"That's what it means, all right. We're going to have to trust God to keep them from doing that."

8
General Forrest
Saves the Day

By the time the Richmond troops arrived at Fort Donelson, Jeff and Tom were worn out. They had ridden part of the way on flat cars but walked the last forty miles. Now, as they sat wearily around a campfire, hugging it for warmth, Jeff said with chattering teeth, "I don't see why we had to come all the way down here, Tom. Seems to me there'd be plenty of fighting going on around Richmond."

"I reckon this is more important than you know, Jeff."

Jeff stared at the old crumbling fort perched on the banks of the Tennessee River. "It don't look like much to me. What's so all-fired important about it?"

Tom blew on his hands, then held them close to the flickering yellow flames. "Well, look here . . ." Picking up a stick, he began to draw in the dirt. "You see, right here—this is the Confederate line. Here it comes across bluegrass country and all the way across Missouri and on to Indian Territory, several hundred miles long. Now all this is under the command of General Albert Sidney Johnston."

"I've heard of him!" Jeff exclaimed. "They say President Davis puts a lot of stock in him."

"That's right. He said once he didn't know about other generals but he knew he had one, and that was Albert Sidney Johnston."

"He ain't as good as Robert E. Lee, I bet," Jeff said loyally. He looked around again. "What about this fort?"

Tom drew more wavy lines. "Well, here's the Tennessee River, and here's the Cumberland. You see, they run side by side until they come toward the Ohio. Now, right here at the Ohio the Union gunboats have been a threat to our line."

"I don't see what difference that makes. A few gunboats couldn't whip all of us Confederates stretching across here, could they?"

"No, but here's what happens. You see this area here—here's where we been getting our supplies. Our armies can't fight if they don't have food and guns and ammunition. Things have been coming to us up this river, and Fort Donelson here is the fort that's supposed to keep us from controlling the supply line."

"Oh! So this is where we have to stop the Yankees. Is that right?"

"That's right." Tom looked out across the fading daylight to where the river purled past the old fort. "If they control the Mississippi, I don't think we can win. And right here at this little place called Donelson, that's where it's going to be settled. If they whip us here, they can take the whole river."

"Well, who's going to be our commanding officer now that we're here? I wish we could have brought General Lee with us."

"Reckon he's got all he can do back in Richmond. From what I hear, McClellan's going to be there soon with about a hundred thousand soldiers. That's why we gotta stop 'em here quick so we can get back to help him."

After only a few days, word came that the Northern general, Grant, had taken Fort Henry just a few miles away.

"I reckon they'll be coming to get us now for sure," Tom said dubiously. "I wish we were anywhere except here. I don't like the generals we've got."

The two generals in charge were General Pillow and General Floyd. When the Federal attack came, these generals held out for two days, but then they caved in.

The first that Jeff heard of the bad news was when Tom came in, his mouth hard. "Well, they've done it! They're gonna surrender."

"Surrender! Why, they can't do that!"

"They're arguing about it now, but the word is that those two are gonna quit."

"What about us, all of us here?"

"We'll wind up in a prison camp, that's what! I had a bad feeling about this all the time, Jeff. Now it looks like I was right."

"We've got to get out of here! We can't stay here. I couldn't stand it in one of those prison camps, and you couldn't either, Tom."

"I know it." Tom's shoulders sagged, and he said grimly, "But I just don't know what we're going to do about it."

* * *

Inside the officers' tent, an argument was going on. The two generals Pillow and Floyd were so discouraged they could do little but moan. Another general, Buckner, tried to encourage them, but they would have none of it.

"You stay here, General Buckner—Pillow and I will leave."

There was a fourth officer in the tent—General Nathan Bedford Forrest. He was a tall, strong-looking man with a full beard and fierce eyes. He had listened to the defeatist talk of Pillow and Floyd and protested that there was still a way out. He could lead the men through the swamp and across the river, through the enemy lines. "I can get us all out, if you'll just listen!"

But General Floyd shook his head. "No, it's hopeless. You can't do it, Forrest. You'll have to surrender your command."

General Forrest glared at him. "I didn't come to this place to surrender my command. You can do what you want, but I am leading my men out of here." He turned and left the tent.

General Forrest went to where his cavalry troop was stationed. The men gathered around to hear him. Tom and Jeff had made friends with one of the troopers, and they looked up at the big general.

Forrest said, "Men, they're going to surrender, but not me. I'm getting out of here if I have to die doing it. Anybody who wants to come is welcome."

At once the cavalrymen let out a shrill yelp and began hurriedly saddling their horses.

Tom nudged Jeff in the ribs. "This is our chance. I'm going to get out of here with General Forrest."

"But we don't have any horses."

"I don't care. We'll swim out if we have to. Come on now."

Tom led the way to where the general was issuing orders. He waited until he was free and then said, "General?"

Forrest turned his dark eyes on him. "Yes? What is it?"

"My brother and I, we don't relish going to a Yankee prison camp. Take us with you."

"I don't have any horses to spare."

"We'll swim—anything. I'd rather die than go to one of those prison camps."

"Me too, General," Jeff piped up. "Our pa's in a Federal hospital now, and he'll be in a prison camp himself soon. All three of us can't go there."

Forrest hesitated only a moment. "All right, I'll see what I can do." He looked around. "Lieutenant Simon, put these two fellows behind a couple of our troopers. They can ride double. "

"Yes, sir!" the lieutenant snapped. Then, as the general turned away, he said, "Come on, fellows! We've got to get out of here. I'll find you somebody to ride with."

An hour later General Forrest's troop rode out. Jeff and Tom rode behind two of the cavalrymen. The icy river came up as high as the horses' bellies, and they held their feet up. The water was cold enough to numb the toes.

The lean cavalryman Jeff was holding onto turned and grinned. "A little bit cold, ain't it?"

"I don't care," Jeff said instantly. "I'll do anything to get out of that place."

"Well, you ought to join the cavalry. It's the only way to fight a war."

Jeff never forgot that ride through the rising, freezing river. A few of the men didn't make it across, but most of them did.

When he and Tom had gotten safely away, Tom thanked the general. "Sir, I guess we better get on back to Richmond. Our outfit's there."

General Forrest nodded. "From what I hear, McClellan's bringing a pretty big bunch out of Washington, headed for Richmond. If I didn't have to stay here and help clean up this mess, I'd go with you."

"We'll never forget what you've done for us, General Forrest," Tom said. "Thanks a lot!"

Forrest was a stern man, but he grinned. "Remember this—if you get there first with the most, you'll always whup 'em."

He turned and galloped away, and Tom said, "Now, there's one real soldier!"

"He sure is." Jeff nodded with admiration. "I wish we had a hundred just like him!"

9

God Will
Take Care of Us

Spring was around the corner in Kentucky as
Leah walked down the muddy road. The mid-April
wind was mild today. Seeing her father over at the
barn, she walked toward him.

He was repairing a piece of harness and looked
up as she came toward him. "Warm today isn't it?
I think spring's here for sure, Pet." He continued to
punch holes in the harness as he spoke. "Be time
for spring planting pretty soon. Always like to see
this time of year come. Seems like God makes everything new."

Leah sat down on a box. Watching him work,
she nodded. "I always look for the first crocus when
they break through the earth," she said. "I know
for sure it's spring then."

"Funny how you can tell weather by things
like that. Like winter. You know winter's not over
until the pecans drop." He grinned at her. "Pecan
trees are a lot smarter than we are sometimes—
about weather anyway."

They sat chatting, and then Leah asked, "Do
you think we'll be going back to Washington soon,
Pa?"

Daniel Carter hesitated, holding the strip of
leather in one hand and the awl in the other. Finally he said, "I reckon so. From what I hear about it,

President Lincoln has told General McClellan that he's gonna have to fish or cut bait."

"The troops all love General McClellan, though," Leah said.

"Well, he's about the best at getting an army ready to fight."

A bluebird lit on a peach tree branch a few feet away. The breeze ruffled his feathers, and he cocked his head to one side and uttered a short querulous syllable, then flew away.

"Just when will we be going back do you think, Pa?"

"I figure about next week." He shook his head sadly. "We won the battle at Shiloh, but we lost many a good man doing it. I don't think any of us on either side were ready for those kinds of losses. They say that Washington's just one big hospital now—even private homes are taking in wounded soldiers."

"I'm glad Royal got back all right," Leah said, "and the last letter from Jeff said there hadn't been any fighting around Richmond."

"Well, there will be. That's straight where McClellan will have to head. Like I started to say, President Lincoln has given him an ultimatum. He'll have to fight or step down."

Leah had been reading the newspaper, and all the headlines said, "Forward to Richmond!"

McClellan had trained his troops well, but he had no respect for the president, whom he called "The Original Gorilla." It was common knowledge that he treated Mr. Lincoln with contempt.

Once during the winter, Lincoln went to see the young general to discuss strategy. When he was told that McClellan was out, the president waited for him for about an hour. McClellan returned and walked by the president without so much as a word. Lincoln waited thirty minutes more, then asked that McClellan be told he was there. The answer came back that the general had gone to bed. Not once but several times, Lincoln tried to see the general and was ignored.

However, the country was in a furor now. After the victory at Shiloh, people were demanding that Richmond be taken. Now everyone in the country —North and South—knew that the huge Army of the Potomac would soon be headed toward the Southern capital.

When Mr. Carter finally finished the work on the harness, he put it aside and said, "Let's go get some hot chocolate—if we can get your mother to make it for us."

"I can make it myself," Leah announced, and they walked across the yard to the house.

They found Sarah playing with little Esther, and she looked up as they came in. "Take care of the baby, will you, Leah? I need to go help Mother with the washing."

"Morena and I will do it, won't we, Morena?"

Morena was wearing a simple white dress, and her face lit up with a smile. She never spoke, but somehow Leah always felt she understood what was being said. She had been told that Morena would never really understand, but she always talked to her as an equal.

"How's baby Esther, Morena?" she asked, picking up the child. She propelled her across the floor as if Esther could walk, and the baby chortled with glee.

Her mother suddenly appeared at the door. "Why don't you give Esther her bath, Leah? Be sure you don't get the water too hot."

"All right, Ma."

For the next half hour, Esther was the object of attention from the family. She loved her bath. She splashed the water and batted her eyes and tasted the soap carefully, then made a face that made them all laugh. She had beautiful rosy skin, and Sarah bent over her, saying, "Lots of women would give everything they own to have a complexion like that."

Esther Majors had been something to tie the Carter family together. They had taken the child because Nelson had no place else to keep her while he was in the army, and they had never regretted their decision.

"Why, she's just like our own," Leah said to her mother. "I'll hate it when Mr. Majors takes her back again."

"I don't know when that will be," her mother had said. "Not till this war's over and he gets out of prison."

After Leah had given Esther her bath, powdered her, and put her into fresh clothing, she surrendered the baby to her mother, who gave her a bottle.

Leah and Sarah prepared lunch, and when they all sat down to eat, Mr. Carter bowed his head and prayed, "Oh, God our Father, we thank Thee for this food and Thy every blessing. Give us health and strength. Protect our men in service. Bring this cruel war to an end. We pray in Jesus' Name. Amen."

At once Leah speared one of the fresh, fluffy biscuits that her mother had made and stuffed it into her mouth.

"Leah! You eat like a starved wolf!" Mrs. Carter protested.

"I don't think she ever tastes anything." Sarah smiled. "You have to taste with your tongue, and she's so busy chewing and swallowing she doesn't have time."

"I eat my vittles the way I like," Leah sniffed. "These are good biscuits."

When they were almost through, Morena looked up suddenly. She had acute hearing, and a few minutes later Leah heard the sound of a horse approaching. She got up and went to a window.

"It's Horace with the mail," she said. "I'll go get it." She ran outside and was back in a moment with a letter. "It's for you, Pa. From Richmond. I don't know the handwriting."

Dan Carter took the envelope, deliberately took his glasses from his pocket, and balanced them on his nose. He stared at the handwriting and said, "I don't recognize it either."

"Well, open it and you'll find out!" Leah's mother said sharply.

"Just what I was going to do." Opening the envelope, Daniel pulled a sheet of paper out, unfolded it, and stared again.

He was silent for so long that his wife said in exasperation, "Well, what is it? Who's it from?"

Daniel removed his glasses and handed the letter over to her. "Comes as quite a surprise. It's from Uncle Silas."

"Uncle *Silas?*" She took the letter from him

and scanned it quickly. "We haven't heard from him for a long time," she murmured.

"Who's Uncle Silas?" Leah asked curiously.

Daniel Carter leaned his elbows on the table. "He's my father's older brother. When I was growing up we had a hard time. For a while it looked like we would almost starve to death. Those were hard days back then. I remember so well. We'd hit bottom and my father was sick and my mother had died a few years before that. We were all just about past hope, but one day a man came riding up. I didn't know him, but my father said, 'Why, that's my brother Silas, from Richmond.'"

"You'd never seen him?" Sarah asked.

"No, we'd heard about him, though, and he sure came like a present from heaven. He evidently had some money, because he paid our bills and got us out of debt and took care of us till Pa got well. Later on, he paid my way in school." Daniel rubbed his chin thoughtfully. "I sure think a lot of Uncle Silas."

"It sounds like he's pretty bad off," Mrs. Carter said, looking up from the letter. "I can hardly read his handwriting, it's so thin and scratchy."

"Is he sick?" Leah asked.

"That's what the letter says—and he's asked if I can come and help him till he gets well."

Silence ran around the table until Sarah said, "That would be hard to do—for you to go to Richmond, I mean. Wouldn't it, Father?"

"I don't know. A man can do what he has to do."

"But then you couldn't do your sutler work if you did that, could you?" Leah asked.

"No, but I've got to do something to help Silas. He gave us hope back when there wasn't any hope."

Mrs. Carter had been studying the letter. "Sounds like he's got some mighty poor nursing. He doesn't say much, but I take it he doesn't have any relatives there to help him."

"No, he's all alone now. He had a sister, but she died a few years ago. She was an invalid, and Uncle Silas took care of her instead of the other way around. He's a mighty good man. A mighty good man."

The family sat there, thoughtful, and it was Sarah who said gently, "Well, Father, we'll just have to pray about it. God is able, isn't He?"

"Yes, Daughter, He is, and that's what we'll do. We'll pray about it."

For the next few days, Dan Carter had little to say. He seemed lost in his thoughts, and his family would notice him just staring off into space.

"He's worried about Uncle Silas," Leah's mother said to her one day. "We've prayed and prayed about it, and still I can't see any way to help. We could send money to hire a nurse, but you never know what you'd get in a case like that."

Leah had said little, but she keenly felt her father's grief over his uncle. She had never seen him quite so disturbed over anything except the war. She tried to talk to him, but he only said again and again, "I've got to help him somehow, Pet. I've got to!"

One night after Leah had gone to bed, she was restless and could not sleep. She was thinking mostly of the problem with her father's uncle in Richmond, and she began to pray. For a long time she lay there asking God to do something to make it possible for her father to help. She tried to think of some way he could go to Richmond, but the more she thought of that the less possible it seemed. She went to sleep praying, *Oh, God, show us some way to help!*

The next morning when Leah woke at the sound of a rooster crowing, she discovered that an idea had taken possession of her. For a time she lay looking out at the tree that brushed its branches against the window pane.

At last she got up, dressed, and went into the dining room. The family was already gathered there, and as Leah sat down she wondered how to say what she had to tell them.

Her father asked the blessing, and Sarah picked up Esther and began shoveling strained peaches into her mouth, cooing at her.

Finally Leah asked, "Pa, you think God tells people what to do?"

"Why—of course, I do! The Bible's full of things like that!" Dan Carter said in surprise. "You know your Bible better than that, Leah. Think about the Lord telling Joseph to take the Baby Jesus to Egypt." He stared at her intently. "Why did you ask a thing like that?"

"Because I think maybe the Lord told me something last night."

Everyone looked at her in surprise.

Her father said, "Well, what is it, Pet?"

"I've been praying and praying about some way to help your Uncle Silas—but I don't see any way that you could go, Pa. In the first place, you need to go back and help the soldiers. That's what God's told you to do, isn't it?"

"It surely is, and that's one thing I've been worried about. If it wasn't for that, I'd go to Richmond like a shot."

"Well, I think God is telling *me* to go help nurse your uncle."

"Why, you can't do that, Leah!" her mother said. "You're just a child!"

"I'm a good nurse, Ma. You know that. If all he needs is somebody to help him until he gets well, I can do it. You know I can."

And then the big argument started that went on all that day and into the next. At first, everyone said that Leah was totally mistaken, that God couldn't have told her to do such a thing. She didn't argue, but by the next day, when they met in the parlor to talk more about it, she had convinced them that she at least *could* care for Uncle Silas.

"But *should* you do it?" her father asked. "That's a long way for a young girl to go. And we don't know anyone there."

"We know Tom and Jeff," Leah said. "They're still stationed in Richmond. They could help."

"But they'll be gone with the army soon," Sarah said. She had been very quiet during all of this, but there was a peculiar look in her eyes. Now she turned to her father and mother. "You know, I think that we'll have to listen to what Leah is saying."

Mrs. Carter looked at her oldest daughter in surprise. "Are you in favor of her going?" She put great faith in Sarah's judgment, for she was a young woman wise beyond her years. "Do you think it would be all right?"

Sarah hesitated, then nodded. "I think it will be all right—as long as I go with her."

Leah cried, "Oh, Sarah, would you?" She ran to her sister, threw her arms around her, and began a little dance. "I knew it would be all right! If you go with me, it has to be!"

Daniel Carter stood looking at his daughters with a worried expression on his face. Then finally he smiled. "Well, I guess I'm not a man to go against what God's telling anybody to do. I'd feel better, though, with the two of you going together."

Leah came over and threw her arms around his neck. "It'll be all right, Pa. You'll see. God will be with us!"

10
Richmond

As soon as the two young women got off the train at Richmond, Leah looked at her sister and laughed. "Your face is so dirty!" she exclaimed. "It's all covered with soot."

Sarah touched her cheek with one finger and stared at the residue on the fingertip. "Well," she said, shaking her head in disgust, "no dirtier than yours. Those coal burning engines really make a mess, don't they?"

As they turned to collect their baggage, a middle-aged man, with one arm missing and wearing parts of a Confederate uniform, came up to say, "Here, ladies, let me help you with your suitcases."

"Why, thank you." Sarah smiled. "Those three large bags and those two small ones right there." The man scurried around and, despite the missing arm, managed the baggage very well. He whistled for a carriage, using two fingers on his surviving hand. "You're going down to the hotel, I guess?"

"No, we're going to 1120 Elm Street."

"That's over on the east side of town. Well, here you go." The wounded soldier cheerfully piled their bags in the back of the buggy that drew up and said to the driver, "Take these two ladies to 1120 Elm Street, Harry."

"Sure will," the driver replied cheerfully. He was a tall, lean man with a shock of white hair, which was revealed when he pulled his hat off. He watched while the soldier helped the two young women in and as Sarah pulled a bill from her purse.

"Will Union greenbacks do?" Sarah asked tentatively. "I don't have any Confederate money yet."

The soldier with one arm grinned and winked at the driver. "Sure will, ma'am. I wish I had my pockets full of those Union greenbacks. You won't have any trouble spending them here in Richmond."

Harry, the driver, said, "I'll take care of them, Perry." He spoke to the horses. "Hup, Babe! Hup, Mame!" and the carriage moved off, the driver threading through the busy traffic.

"Perry lost that arm at Bull Run," he said, "but I guess he's better off than those that didn't make it back at all." He greeted several people as they made their way along the bustling street that seemed clogged with civilians and soldiers, horses, buggies, and wagons.

"Pretty busy town, Richmond. You ladies come from around here?"

"From Kentucky," Sarah said.

That seemed safe enough, Leah thought. Kentucky was one of those border states controlled by neither the North nor the South.

"Come for a visit?" the inquisitive driver asked, his sharp eyes turning to examine them.

Leah saw no harm in saying, "Yes, our father's uncle is quite ill. My sister and I have come to see if we could help nurse him. His name is Silas Carter. I don't suppose you know him?"

"Well, no, ma'am, I don't—but with two pretty young nurses like you, I don't reckon he'll have any trouble getting well." The driver grinned and slapped the backs of the horses with the line. "Get up there, you lazy hosses!"

They passed through the main part of town and then through what seemed to be an industrial district. "What's that big building right over there?" Leah asked. "The one with smoke coming out of the chimneys?"

"Oh, that's the Tredgar Iron Works, missy. Turns out most of the cannons for the army. Lots of folks work in there. Reckon you could get jobs if you wanted them. But I guess you will have all you can do with your nursing."

The trip did not take long, for the house was located just on the border of Richmond. The driver drew up before a tall, two-storied house, white with gingerbread carvings across the front and a wide porch.

"Here we are, 1120 Elm Street. Let me help you ladies with your things," the driver said. He hopped down, assisted them to the ground, then turned back for the baggage.

They paid the driver, then walked up onto the front porch and knocked.

Almost at once—so quickly that Leah suspected the woman who answered the door must have been looking out the window—the door swung open. A middle-aged woman with sharp features and a frown said, "Yes? What do you want?"

Leah was a little taken aback by the abruptness of the greeting.

"Why, I'm Sarah Carter, and this is my sister, Leah. We've come to see my father's Uncle Silas."

"Well, he's sick. He can't see no one."

The door started to close.

Sarah's face flushed, and she stepped forward and put her foot in the doorway. "I'm sorry, but we'll have to see my uncle. Who are you? Are you the housekeeper?"

"I'm the nurse, Mrs. Watkins, and I tell you the doctor don't want no one seeing Mr. Carter!"

Sarah's mouth went firm, and her eyes half shut. She was a mild-mannered girl, but she recognized insolence when she saw it. "Mrs. Watkins, I'm telling you right now, we've come to take care of my uncle. Now you can either let us in, or we'll go get the authorities, who will see to it. Now which will it be?"

The sharp-faced woman hesitated. She gave them a baleful look and then said, "Well, you can come in for a little while, I suppose." She stepped back. "He's down here in this room, and you can't stay long. He don't feel like seeing visitors."

Sarah and Leah exchanged glances, and Sarah gave her head a warning shake. They followed the gray-haired woman down a short hall. When she opened a door, they stepped inside.

Mrs. Watkins said, "There's two women here claim to be your kin. You don't want to see them, do you?"

Sarah looked across the room to see a thin-faced man with snow-white hair lying in a bed. Two pillows propped him up. His face was pale, and his mouth was drawn tight in an invalid's look, but his eyes were bright blue and took them in carefully.

"Why, you must be Dan's girls!" he said in surprise. "Come in! Come in!"

"Yes, I'm Sarah, and this is Leah."

They walked to the bed and shook hands with the elderly man. His hand, Leah thought, felt like a bird's bones, it was so fragile. She smiled, saying,

"Pa wanted us to come and take care of you till you're feeling better, Uncle Silas."

"I'll do all the taking care of he needs," Mrs. Watkins said. She stood there with an angry look on her face. "He's a sick man, and he doesn't need anybody fussing with him."

"I think that'll be enough, Mrs. Watkins," Sarah said firmly. "You may go now."

The woman's mouth dropped open. Evidently she was not accustomed to being challenged.

Sarah said, "We won't be needing you for a while. I'll talk with you later to see if it will be possible for you to stay on. Shut the door on your way out."

Mrs. Watkins gasped, and her face flushed. "Well, I never!" she muttered, then turned and left, slamming the door so that the pictures on the wall trembled.

Suddenly Silas Carter laughed aloud. It was not a hearty laugh, and his voice seemed rusty as though he had not used it much, but he was smiling, and his eyes twinkled. "Well, dog my cat! I never seed the beat of that! That woman's had me buffaloed, Sarah, but I can see you know how to handle her."

"Who *is* she?" Sarah asked. "She doesn't seem like very good company for someone who's not well."

"She's the awfulest pest I ever ran across," Silas Carter said, "but she's all I could get. Her and that sister of hers, who's worse." He looked up hopefully. "Are you girls here for just a short stay?"

"No, we're here till you get well, Uncle Silas," Sarah said at once. Looking sharply into his face, she said, "Would you like for me to tell Mrs. Watkins and her sister they won't be needed anymore?"

"Would I! That would be a blessing!" The old man groaned. "Here!" He fumbled in the drawer of the bedside table and brought out a purse. "I owe them for this week. Pay them and tell them thank you and never to come back again."

Leah laughed. "It's a good thing we came, Uncle Silas. I don't think you'd have lasted long with those two."

"Leah—that's your name, is it?" Uncle Silas said. "Well, you're right about that, girl. Hope you two can cook better than they can. They could make a tenderloin steak taste like a piece of shoe leather."

"Oh, we can both cook real good," Leah said. "You go fire those two women, Sarah, and I'll stay here and talk to Uncle Silas."

Sarah took the purse, asked the amount owed the women, and then left the room. As soon as she was gone, Silas drew a deep breath and seemed to settle. "I was never so glad to see anybody in all my born days. Now, you tell me all about my nephew, Dan, and your ma and all about your family."

Leah sat beside the bed and talked to him cheerfully, stopping once to open the window, pull back the drapes, and let sunlight flood the room.

Uncle Silas seemed fascinated by every detail, and when Leah mentioned they had two friends in the Confederate army, he looked at her quizzically.

"Well, that's something, ain't it! Tell me more about these young fellers."

Sarah came in as Leah was still talking about Jeff and Tom. She stood at the bedside for a moment, and then, when she found a place to interrupt, she said, "Well, the Watkins sisters are not happy, but you'll not have to see them anymore, Uncle Silas. Now, what would you like for supper?"

"Ice cream and cake"—he grinned— "but I'll take whatever I can get. Just surprise me." He looked closely at Sarah. "What's that about this young feller Tom that's stuck on you? Tom Majors, is it?"

A flush touched Sarah's cheek, and she cast an irritated look at Leah. "We're just good friends."

"You are not," Leah spoke up. "He wants to marry you. That's not just good friends."

"Hush, Leah." Then she laughed. "I see our family will have no secrets from you, Uncle Silas. Well, I'll go fix supper. Leah, come see to our things. Where do you want us to put them, Uncle Silas?"

When the girls were outside, Leah said, "It's a good thing we came. Those two women would have driven a saint crazy."

"Well, you go up and put our things away and then come help me with supper. We can talk about how we're going to divide our duties up later on tonight."

Sarah watched until her younger sister had ascended the stairs, carrying a suitcase, and then turned to the kitchen. As she began pulling groceries off the shelves to prepare the meal, she looked out the window. A soldier in a gray uniform walked by, and her heart jumped.

Then she laughed at herself. If you're going to think every Confederate soldier you see is Tom Majors, you'll go crazy!

Still, from time to time, she'd look out the window and examine the soldiers who walked by.

* * *

"Look what I got! Look what I got!"

Tom Majors had been cleaning his musket, and he glanced up with a blink of surprise as Jeff came running across the field waving a sheet of paper. "Look! Read this, Tom!"

"What is it? We done won the war?" Tom asked, grinning at his younger brother. He took the paper and then stood up abruptly, dropping the musket. "Is this right? Is this true?"

"That's what it says, isn't it? Leah and Sarah are here in Richmond to take care of their pa's uncle. Look! There's the address. And what's more, we're invited to supper."

Tom grinned broadly and could not seem to stop staring at the paper. "Well, I'll be a swaggletailed duck! I would have thought of anything but this."

He glanced up quickly and saw Lieutenant Ormsby walking by. "Jeff, you wait here. I'm going to talk the lieutenant into letting us go into town tonight."

"Be sure I go with you," Jeff called after him. He stood waiting, anxiously shifting from one foot to the other.

After a short conversation, Tom came back.

"Did he say it was all right?"

"He said I'd have to stand an extra watch, but that's all right. Come on! Let's get our best clothes on and get to town."

By the time they had their best uniforms on and had made the trip to Richmond, the shadows were beginning to lengthen. They had walked until they caught a ride with an army supply wagon, so

102

they were dusty when they arrived at the tall white house.

"There it is," Tom said. "See that number?" He ran up the steps, followed quickly by Jeff, and knocked on the door.

It opened almost at once, and Leah came out, her face beaming. "Tom! Jeff! Boy, I'm so glad to see you!" She threw herself at Tom and hugged him. Then when he released her, she looked at Jeff.

Jeff's face grew crimson. As glad as he was to see her, he just stuck his hand out as he would to another boy. "Well, hey, good to see you," he mumbled.

"Oh, Jeff!" Leah cried and gripped his hand hard.

Then Sarah was at the door. She was wearing a pink and brown, oversized, checked gingham dress with puffed sleeves. There were satin ribbons fastened with a brooch to hold each sleeve tightly, and her dark blue eyes were fixed on Tom as she whispered, "Hello, Tom—so good to see you." She put out her hand. Tom took it, and she said, "Ouch! Not so hard!"

Tom was wearing Confederate gray with a campaign cap, which he pulled off, allowing his dark hair to fall over his forehead. "Sorry, Sarah. I'm just so all-fired glad to see you, you and Leah both! What in the world are you doing here?"

Sarah explained their mission, then said, "Come on in and meet Uncle Silas."

Their uncle was sitting in a wheelchair in the parlor. When the two tall soldiers were introduced, he put out his hand. "Glad to meet both of you. I want to tell you, these two young women have about saved my life."

Tom grinned broadly. "I tell you what, we're glad to see them too, aren't we, Jeff?"

"Sure are," Jeff muttered. He was happier to see Leah than he'd ever thought. She was wearing a pink dress trimmed with blue ribbons, and her hair was parted away from the center and tied back the way older women did theirs. He wanted to say how pretty she looked, but he was too bashful for that.

"Well," Sarah said, "you men get acquainted while Leah and I finish setting the table. Supper'll be ready in a few moments."

She left with Leah, and Silas plied the two soldiers with questions. When he had their story, he said, "So you grew up friends with my nephew, Dan." He shook his head, "I haven't seen much of Dan lately. I sure think the world of him though."

"So do we, sir," Tom said. "I guess Leah and Sarah told you how their family has taken our sister to raise."

"Why, no, I didn't hear about that."

"Yes, our ma died when the baby was born. Esther's her name. We couldn't take care of her—all three of us in the army. So Mr. Carter and his wife, they sent a letter saying they'd keep Esther till we were able. So that's where she is—in Pineville."

"That's just like something Dan would do. Mary too. That pair is mighty special," Silas said. He fixed his bright blue eyes on Tom. "I guess it's a little bit hard on you, isn't it? I mean, being in the Confederate army and some of your friends back home, such as the Carters, being on the other side."

Tom took a deep breath, then released it. There was sorrow in his eyes. "I guess there are folks all over this country torn apart like us. But I don't think of the Carters as Yankees—they're just friends and neighbors. I guess that's what Mr. Lincoln meant when he said we must not be enemies. We're one people. After this is over I hope it will be that way again."

At that point, Leah came in. "All right, time to eat!" She went behind Silas's chair and pushed him into the dining room. "Now, you sit here by me, Jeff, and you can sit over there by Sarah, Tom."

Jeff grinned. "You've gotten real bossy, haven't you? Who died and made you queen?" Nevertheless, he sat down.

Silas said, "I reckon we'll have the blessing, if you boys don't mind." He said a quick prayer and then looked up over the food and took a deep breath. "Well, this is something. You fellows pitch in. You girls too, and I'll show you how a sick man can start to get well."

Food was not yet in short supply in Richmond. They had pork chops and beans and sweet potatoes and fried chicken for the main meal, with fluffy biscuits and glasses of frothy white milk.

Afterward, when Sarah brought out a peach pie, Tom groaned. "Why didn't you tell me you had peach pie, Sarah? You know that's my favorite, and I didn't save room for it."

"That's all right. I did," Jeff said. "I can eat yours."

But Tom rapped his hand and told him to mind his own business.

After the meal they sat around talking for a while, but very soon Uncle Silas grew tired, and Sarah went to help him into bed. "Come on, Jeff,

I'll show you around the neighborhood," Leah offered.

"All right." Jeff got up, and the two went outside.

They walked along the streets of Richmond. Leah pointed out various trees and birds' nests she'd already spotted. The air was calm now and getting cooler. The moan of doves was in the air.

"I like that sound, don't you? It reminds me of home."

"Yes, it is nice." Suddenly Jeff said, "Say, Leah, I'm sure glad you're here. How long are you going to stay?"

"I don't know," she said, pleased to hear Jeff admit he was glad to see her. "We'll have to stay until Uncle Silas gets well—or well enough to get along without nursing. Now tell me all about Fort Donelson. Did you see any of the fighting?"

As they walked along, he told her the story of the fall of Donelson and how they had escaped with General Forrest and made their way back to Richmond.

Listening, she thought, *My, he seems to have gotten taller in just the short while since I saw him. He's going to be as tall as his father, I bet—and maybe as good looking.*

Inside the house Sarah returned to find Tom looking at the pictures on the parlor wall. "Where did Leah and Jeff get off to?" she asked.

"They're out looking at birds' nests, I suppose —trying to find an ostrich egg. You know how they are." Tom came over and stood close. "I've missed you," he said simply.

106

Her cheeks flushed, and she looked very pretty. "I've missed you too." Then hastily she added, "Come along. We can go for a walk too—before it gets too dark. Uncle Silas will be all right." They walked outside, saw Jeff and Leah far down the block, and followed them slowly.

He talked about the army. "You know, Richmond's not the safest place for you to be now, Sarah. Everybody in the North and South knows General McClellan's coming with the Army of the Potomac. Word is, he's ready to come. You'll be trapped here in Richmond—a city under siege."

Sarah said nothing for a moment. Then she murmured, "It's all right, Tom. We know that God told us to come here, so He'll take care of us. Now let me tell you about Esther." She told about all the things that the baby had done, how sweet she was, how she looked. "I wish I had a picture of her. She's the sweetest baby I've ever seen. It was a real blessing when she came to be with us. Even Morena is taken by her."

By now they had nearly caught up to Jeff and Leah.

"Are you still trusting God about your pa?" Leah asked.

Jeff had noticed his brother and Sarah approaching. He quickly said, "Well, I'm still praying. I got to admit getting him out of prison doesn't look very possible, but I'm not giving up."

"I guess it's never easy to follow God, Jeff. But the two of us, we'll never give up!"

11
Sarah's Admirer

If Tom and Jeff had had their way, they would have been back to the home of Silas Carter every day. However, General McClellan had landed his troops, and they were moving up the peninsula, straight for Richmond. Every available man was brought together by General Joe Johnston for the defense of the city, so the two young men were kept busy.

Leah complained one day to Sarah, "I don't see why they won't let Tom and Jeff come and see us—at least once in a while. Just the two of them won't make any difference to the old army!"

Sarah looked up from the peas she was shelling, dropping them into a bowl in her lap. "I've never seen any people as serious as these, Leah. They know if they don't stop General McClellan and the Northern army, the war will be over for them." She slit one of the pea pods, slipped a finger in the gap, and the peas drummed into the bottom of the bowl. "In a way I wish it would be like that. All I can think of is that somewhere in that army our brother's got a part. I don't sleep well thinking about him."

"And about Tom too, and Jeff." Leah nodded. "I know what you mean." She looked down at the peas in her own bowl. "I hate shelling peas. I think sometimes I'd rather dig a ditch."

"You like to eat them well enough. You're going to be fat as a pig if you keep on eating so much. You're growing up to be a big girl anyway."

Leah flushed. She was still self-conscious about her height. At thirteen she was already almost as tall as Sarah, who was seventeen. "Well, I may be a giant in height," she said, "but I'll never be fat. I'll see to that!"

Later in the morning, a note came in the mail. It was addressed to Silas.

Their uncle opened it as soon as Leah handed it to him. He scanned the message quickly and said, "Well, you girls are going up in society it looks like."

"What do you mean, Uncle Silas?"

"This is an invitation from Mrs. Mary Chesnut. She's one of the social leaders in Richmond. Her husband is President Davis's military adviser." He scanned the note again. "She wants you and Sarah to come to a tea she's having tomorrow afternoon."

"But we don't know her," Leah said. "How would she know about us?"

"Oh, I've got a few friends high up, and I've told them—and I suppose they've told Mrs. Chesnut. She's a very kind lady. Her husband and I did some business together more than once. So get your best dresses out because you're just liable to run into anybody at her house—maybe even the president, or General Lee."

"Not General Lee, I bet," Leah said. "He's out getting the soldiers ready for the battle. I'll go tell Sarah."

The two girls were excited about the Chesnuts' tea. At 2:00 the next afternoon they went in a carriage at Silas's insistence. The Chesnut home was a large, two-story house in one of the better sections of town. Carriages lined the street outside, and Leah said, "My gracious, it looks like everybody in town is here. I never saw such a crowd for a tea party."

The two girls dismounted from the carriage and walked inside, where they were met by a tall, dark-haired lady, very attractive and with a warm smile.

"I'm Mary Chesnut, and you must be Silas Carter's nieces." She took their names and said, "Come now, let me introduce you around."

The two girls soon had their heads swarming with names. The room was full of officers in ash-gray uniforms with shiny brass buttons and black leather boots. It was not long before Sarah had attracted a small group of them around her. Her dark hair and dark eyes and attractive figure drew them like bees.

Mary Chesnut stopped beside Leah, who was sitting off to one side watching her sister. She said, "Your sister is very attractive. She's going to have lots of admirers, I think. There are so many men and not enough ladies to go around."

"I'd think they'd all be off getting ready for the battle."

Mrs. Chesnut had a smooth forehead, but it wrinkled now with a distinct sign of worry. She touched one pearl earring. "Yes, there will be fighting soon, so my husband says."

She spoke for a while of the battle that was to come, and Leah could see that this gracious lady was very concerned indeed.

Finally Mrs. Chesnut glanced again at Sarah, who had been taken over, it seemed, by a young captain. Mrs. Chesnut said with a smile, "It looks like your sister has made a conquest. That's Captain Wesley Lyons. He's the son of one of the wealthiest men in Virginia. Half the young women in Richmond, if not all, have set their cap for him."

"He's nice looking," Leah admitted, taking in the young man's tall form. Lyons had a wealth of brown hair that lay neatly on his head and a trim beard. "But I don't think my sister would be very interested in him."

Mrs. Chesnut gave Leah a curious smile. "Surely every young woman is interested in an attractive, wealthy young man. Why wouldn't your sister be interested?"

Leah hesitated, then said, "She's—she's already interested in a young man." When Mrs. Chesnut gave her an inquiring glance, Leah felt she was getting out of her depth. "But he's joined the Confederate army, and we're Union. My brother is in the Army of the Potomac."

Mrs. Chesnut was a sensitive woman and said, "Oh, my dear! That must be very hard for you and for your sister. So many families are like that, some even here in Richmond—their sons and brothers have gone to fight for the Union. Such a time!"

* * *

In the meanwhile Sarah found herself besieged by the young captain. He was, she saw, accustomed to having his own way with young women, and she thought, *My, he's fine looking—but spoiled to the bone! Any man as rich and good looking as he is probably never heard a woman say no. But Captain Wesley Lyons is going to have to hear that—at least from me.*

111

Lyons was balancing a small teacup on his knee as the two sat together. "You must allow me to show you around Richmond, Miss Carter. I've lived here most of my life, and if you've never been here there are many fine sights to see."

Sarah smiled but said rather pointedly, "I understand there is a battle to be fought very soon. Won't you be involved in that, Captain Lyons?"

"I wish you would call me Wesley," he said. Then he shrugged his shoulders. "I suppose I'll be involved. I'm working with the Quartermaster Corps right now." He seemed defensive about that. "People make fun of us because we don't fight on the front line, but if the soldiers didn't get uniforms and guns and food, what fighting would they do?"

"I'm sure you do a fine job," Sarah said. She avoided the issue of his coming to call, but finally by sheer perseverance he wore her down, and she agreed that he might come.

She was not too surprised when, the next day, Captain Lyons arrived and invited her to go for a drive around the streets of Richmond.

As she got ready, a thought came to Sarah. She was putting on her bonnet when suddenly she looked over at Leah, sitting beside her dressing table and chatting. "Leah, I want you to go with us."

"Me! Why, he didn't come to call on me, Sarah."

"I know that." Sarah adjusted the bonnet and looked at herself critically. "I don't really want to see him, and perhaps having a pesky younger sister along will scare him off." She came over and tousled Leah's blonde hair. "I know how pesky you can be when you want to—so just outdo yourself this afternoon, will you? Make yourself absolutely obnoxious."

Leah said indignantly, "I am not pesky, but just to show you, I will be today."

Leah kept her word, to the captain's sorrow. When they got into the carriage, she planted herself firmly between Captain Lyons and Sarah, then turned and winked at her sister. All afternoon she kept herself between the two, talking non-stop and driving the young captain crazy.

Leah enjoyed the outing because she enjoyed puncturing the ego of Captain Wesley Lyons. However, things ended on a depressing note.

They were driving down Elm Street when Sarah noticed a crowd filing into a large, red brick building. "What's that, Captain?"

"Oh, nothing much," he said. "Just a slave auction."

Sarah gave Leah a sudden look, and somehow Leah knew what her sister was thinking. Both of them had grown up in a state that had slaves, but Pineville had fewer than most. In fact, there was strong Union sentiment in Pineville, and most slave owners had gotten rid of their slaves.

"Let's go inside," Leah said impulsively. "I've never seen a slave auction."

"Oh, I don't think you'd be interested. It's not for little girls," Lyons said pompously.

This, of course, made Leah more determined. She enlisted Sarah's aid, and finally Captain Lyons shrugged and said, "All right, we can at least look inside."

As they walked in, Leah saw a poster proclaiming that a firm named Johnson and Kelly was conducting a sale of Negroes. The room was large, perhaps fifty feet square. It had no furniture except for a few scattered benches and chairs. The white-washed walls were about twelve feet high, and a pair of steep staircases led to the floor overhead. A single door at the back apparently opened to another room.

Leah had heard about slave auctions, of course. The abolitionists preached loudly about the evils of selling human beings, and she agreed with them, although she disliked some of their manners.

Now, as she looked around, she saw that there were two classes of people at the auction, and they might have belonged to separate worlds. Many men were dressed in dark suits and wore broad-brimmed hats and smoked so many cigars that the air was blue. The second group was the blacks, who were either standing along a wall or sitting on benches.

Leah looked closely at one young girl no older than she and saw the fear in her large brown eyes. Pity welled up in her, and she wondered, *What would I be feeling if I were going to be sold and be made into somebody's slave?*

The room was noisy with the talk of the auctioneer, the sellers, and the buyers. At the front was a small, raised platform. As Leah watched, the auctioneer called up one of the black women, wearing a red dress with a white apron.

The auctioneer began to speak. "Now look here, gentlemen, this is a prime specimen. Only nineteen years old, never had a sick day. She's healthy and ready to breed, so what am I offered?"

The bidding started at $1,500 but rose rapidly. The young woman was a mulatto—part white— and very pretty. She dropped her head as the bidding went on, and once a man stepped up on the platform and grasped her jaw. He forced her to open her mouth and examined her teeth. He ran his hand over her body and then stepped down and raised the bid.

The woman was sold for $4,200, and Sarah heard a man nearby say, "That's Thomas from New Orleans. He buys all the pretty ones for his saloons there."

Leah had a sickening feeling in her stomach, and she glanced at Sarah, who nodded.

They both stood it for a while longer, but then a mother was sold to one buyer and fought to keep her little girl with her. As the mother was cuffed into submission, the little girl was picked up bodily by a rough-looking man and carried out of the building, screaming.

Sarah said, "Take us out of here, Captain. I've had enough of this."

When they were in the carriage, Sarah said, "I think I'd like to go home now."

Captain Lyons gave her a surprised look. "Why? Aren't you feeling well?"

Sarah hesitated, then said, "I've never seen a slave auction before. It—it's very disturbing."

"Now you must remember they're not like us," Lyons said. He shrugged his shoulders indifferently. "You can't make anything out of a black but a slave. They don't have souls, you know."

"They do so!" Leah piped up. "I looked into that little girl's eyes, and she was scared, just like I'd be."

Lyons was obviously displeased. "Don't go comparing yourself to them, Leah," he said. "I tell you, they don't know any better, and they're happy enough as they are."

Afterward when Sarah and Leah were alone in their room, they talked about it. "I can't believe anyone could be as blind as that man. To say that those poor people don't know any better. They know they're slaves, all right. Did you see the hopelessness in their eyes?" Sarah spoke angrily.

"Well," Leah said slowly, "I guess that's partly what this war is all about. They talk about states' rights—" she hesitated "—but I think most of our men are fighting to see that nobody belongs to anybody else."

12

Lieutenant Lyons
Smells a Rat

Lieutenant Wesley Lyons was not accustomed to being rejected by young women. His wealth, if not his good looks, would have assured his success with many. Perhaps this was why he saw as a challenge Sarah Carter's refusal to accept him as a suitor. Also he took considerable ribbing from his fellow officers over the young woman's failure to fall under his advances.

"I think she's just got good sense, Wes," Major Rhodes said. He had watched the pursuit of Sarah Carter by his younger junior officer. He had little use for Lyons, and it delighted him that the captain had fallen flat on his face. "I think you'd better give up and find another target for your love affairs," he gibed. "Miss Carter, obviously, wants nothing to do with you."

A flush came to Lyons's cheeks. Angrily he said, "You just wait, Major. I haven't begun to court that girl yet. You'll see! I'll have her or die trying."

It appeared that he might do the latter. Day after day he besieged Sarah with notes, sent flowers, stopped by the house at least three or four times a week, and did everything a young man could do. Still, as polite as Sarah was, she showed no signs of falling under his spell.

* * *

Silas Carter watched the courtship with interest.

He'd become genuinely fond of his two nieces and had grown stronger under their fine nursing. They were both good cooks, and there was something highly satisfying about the way they fussed over him. Silas had been a widower for many years. He had missed his wife terribly. They had not had children, so he was alone in the world. Now his house, instead of being plagued by the two ogres he had hired as nurses, was cheerful. Every day the shades were open, allowing the sun to come in. Leah, somehow, found fresh flowers that brightened the room. There was always the sound of laughter and happy talk.

"By gum," Silas muttered to himself one day as he sat nibbling a piece of Leah's gingerbread, "I didn't know how good life could be! I'd have gotten sick before this if I'd known I'd get such good care."

A little later he said as much to Leah, who reached over and pinched his arm. "You're just trying to get more sympathy, Uncle Silas." She grinned at him. "I never did see a man that didn't like being made over."

"I guess you're right." Silas helped himself to another piece of gingerbread. Then, after swallowing hugely, he said, "You two girls have made a big difference to me. I think I'd have been pushing up daisies now if I'd had to put up with those two monsters any longer."

"Well, I'm glad you're better, but you're a long way from well yet. So you're going to have to put up with us for a while."

"That's fine with me." Uncle Silas nodded vigorously. Then he looked out the window and saw Sarah coming, carrying a basket. She had gone to the store to buy some groceries, and now, as she approached, she had her head down, apparently studying the sidewalk.

Silas asked, "How's that romance coming along between Sarah and that captain?"

"Oh, he's going to pester her to death!" Leah's lips turned down in a frown. "I wish he'd go away and leave her alone. She's done everything but hit him with a stick."

"I reckon he's just not used to girls who don't fall over themselves for him. Spoiled like a pup, ain't he now?"

"I think that's right, Uncle Silas."

"She's right took with Tom Majors. I could see that right off."

Leah sighed heavily and reached for a piece of gingerbread. She chewed on it thoughtfully. "I expect they'd be married by now if the war hadn't come along. She says it would just be too hard to be married to anybody in the Confederate army— with our brother in the Union army. I expect right now he's with McClellan, coming up to fight."

"You still keeping up writing a letter every day to Nelson Majors in that hospital in Washington?"

"Well, he gets so lonesome up there. I know a letter means a lot to him. He can't write too much to me. They don't care much about sending letters from Confederate prisoners, I guess, but my pa tells me he went by every day until he left with the army."

"Your pa's following after the Union army as a sutler."

119

"Yes, and I'd be with him, if I weren't here to help you. Pa feels like the Lord's told him to be a sutler. And it *is* nice, because the soldiers are always so grateful when we give them the Scripture and tracts. Seems like they read everything. Some of them are so young. They don't seem much older than I am—though they are, of course."

When Sarah came in and started to put the groceries away, Leah left her uncle and went in to help. "Did you get everything on the list?"

"No, the stores are out of some things already, and the prices are terrible. Confederate money is already going down in value, and it's going to go down more. It's a good thing we brought plenty of greenbacks with us. They fight over them, you know. I'm getting to where I won't take the change in Confederate. I just get more supplies to use it up. One of our dollars is worth twenty of theirs already."

It was as though the Federal government had thrown a massive wall around the South. By sea they formed a blockade of ships. But the Federal navy was small, and there were plenty of blockade runners. These little boats would scoot out after dark, make a run to one of the islands where they would receive stores of all sorts, then dodge back in. They were light craft that drew less water than the Federal gunboats and could easily outrun them. However, every day more gunboats arrived, and the blockade runners were finding it more difficult. And since the fall of Fort Henry, supplies were not coming in from Tennessee and the northern part of the Confederacy.

Sarah put the last of the food on the shelves. "At the beginning of the war, General Scott said the North would have to have a plan to strangle the South—and it looks like that's what we're doing."

"Was there any word about where the Federal army is?"

"No, just that they're on their way and coming very slowly. Everybody says McClellan's a very cautious general, so General Johnson and the other Southern generals are having plenty of time to put up a good defense. Still, they say the Army of the Potomac has over a hundred thousand men—more than twice what the Confederates have."

The two talked for a while and then were delightfully surprised when Jeff and Tom arrived unexpectedly.

"We begged off for leave in town for a day," Jeff said to Leah as they came into the house. "We'll have to do extra duty for it, but I don't care. Come on, let's go out and see if we can find a place to fish. We can go down to the James River maybe."

When they told Silas their plan, he said, "You'll find some fishing poles and lines out in the storage house. Used to go myself quite a bit. A mess of fish wouldn't go bad."

Jeff and Leah made their way to the James, a stream that wound around like a snake. When they got under the shade of a huge hickory, they baited up with the big night crawlers they had found in Uncle Silas's backyard.

Jeff watched Sarah put the hook through a worm, ignoring its squirming. He grinned at her. "I remember when you nearly fainted when you baited a hook. I think you're getting callous now that you're an older woman."

Leah was wearing a plain brown dress, but the sun had given her cheeks an attractive, golden glow. She made a face at him. "I can put a worm on a hook as good as you can, Jeff Majors! I can catch more fish too."

"We'll see about that! I never saw the day a girl could beat me at anything."

They fished for three hours, and at the end of that time Jeff was rather embarrassed.

"I've got six. How many do you have, Jeff?" she asked mischievously.

"Well, I've been fishing in the wrong place. You got where they all are," he grumbled.

"Never mind that. How many did you get?"

"Actually, when I get this one and the next one, I'll have two." Jeff grinned. He lifted out her stringer and shook his head. "What did you do to catch these fish?"

"I always spit on the bait." Leah laughed. "I bet you forgot that, didn't you?"

"Sure did. Well, anyhow, we've got enough here to feed all of us. Let's get on home."

As they walked homeward they talked about the days when they'd hunted and fished together back in Kentucky. And Jeff spoke of his father. He still hadn't quite given up hope, although he was despondent.

When they got near the house, Leah said, "Oh, rats!"

"What's the matter?"

"Look! He's here again!"

"Who's here again?"

"Oh, that Wesley Lyons. He keeps trying to court Sarah."

"I know," Jeff said. "And he'd better be careful. Tom's about ready to stop his clock."

"He can't do that! If he hit an officer, he'd go to jail, or wherever they put soldiers that hit officers."

"Well, he's pretty hot-tempered, Tom is. Come on, we'd better get inside, because I might have to pull him off."

When they got into the house, they found Sarah on the couch, wedged firmly between the two young men. The captain seemed stiff, and Leah sensed at once that he was incensed at having to compete with a mere sergeant.

Quickly she said, "We caught enough fish for supper." Then she glanced at the captain. "But no extra, I guess. Just enough for the five of us."

She was inviting him not to stay for supper. He tried to ignore her.

Then Jeff said, "Miss Sarah, you want to come out and see these fish? Your sister caught them all. I couldn't do a thing today."

Sarah had been very uncomfortable.

When the captain arrived, he had tried to intimidate Tom, using his rank. Tom, however, had gritted his teeth and kept a pleasant expression on his face. He had not, however, offered to leave.

By now Sarah was almost at her wit's end. She had shown them the pictures in the family album. They had carried on such small talk as they could, but she was glad now to rise and say, "Oh, yes! Come along, we'll all go see them."

When they got outside, Leah held up the string of fish, all fine, blue channel cat, weighing anywhere from a pound and a half to two pounds. "I like to eat these," she said, "but they sure are a pain to clean." She looked over at the captain mischievously. "Would you like to help us clean the fish? You can gut 'em, and I'll skin 'em."

"No, thank you," Captain Lyons said. Clearly he was seething inwardly and could not take teasing at all. Finally he said, "I'll stop by and see you later. It seems to be a little crowded right now." He strode off toward the front yard.

As soon as he was gone, Tom said, "I thought he'd never leave."

"You weren't very polite to him," Sarah said. "I thought once he'd have you put under arrest." But she smiled, and the dimples came to her cheeks. Then she laughed out loud. "Oh, I'm glad you came. I'm so tired of him, I could scream." She looked over at Jeff and Leah. "You two, clean those fish. I'll go inside and get ready to cook them. We'll have a good fish supper."

"Be sure you make lots of hush puppies," Leah said. "You can't eat fish without hush puppies. And fried potatoes too."

After supper Sarah, Leah, Tom, and Jeff sat on the porch and talked. Uncle Silas was well enough to join them, and he said after a time, "You don't know how fine this is for me to have family around me. I've been a lonely old man. I don't know how I'll put up with myself when you girls leave."

At the mention of their leaving, a frown crossed Tom's face. He soon found an excuse to go for a walk with Sarah in the falling twilight.

As soon as they were out of hearing of the house, he said, "Sarah, you've got to marry me! I love you more than any man ever loved a woman." He made an impassioned plea, but, as he had expected, it all went for nothing.

"I love you too, Tom," Sarah said gently, "but marriage is forever. It's hard enough for a young man and a young woman to get along and make a good marriage when things are right, and now things are all wrong."

"I love you, and that's not wrong," Tom insisted.

Sarah said nothing for a while. They just walked, and she allowed him to take her hand.

By now darkness had almost completely fallen. He put his arms around her, held her tightly for a moment, and smelled the fragrance of her hair.

Sarah was so lonely and upset that she clung to him, obviously trying to keep the tears back.

He looked down into her face. "Marry me, Sarah." And he kissed her.

After only a moment, she drew back. "No, it can't be. Not for now. Let's go back, Tom. We'll just have to wait."

* * *

But Wesley Lyons was not waiting. He had been infuriated and humiliated by the encounter with a mere sergeant, who seemed to be having success with Sarah Carter.

When he got to his office the next morning, he instructed Lieutenant Smith, "I want you to find out all you can about the Carters. Something's funny about them, I tell you."

"What do you mean, Captain?" the lieutenant asked. "What's funny?"

"Well, they all come from Kentucky, and you know that's all Yankees up there—most of them anyhow. I found out that this sergeant that Sarah

125

Carter's interested in is Tom Majors. He came down from the North—from Kentucky—and joined our army, but I think some of them could be spying for the Union."

"Oh, that doesn't seem likely, does it, Captain? Silas Carter is a good strong Southern supporter."

"They may be putting it over on the old man. It just seems funny to me. Anyway, I want you to look into it. I smell a rat about the whole thing."

"Yes, sir, I'll see to it."

Wesley Lyons leaned back and smiled. "Yes, sir," he said, "I smell a rat. Something abnormal about any young woman that would turn me down for a mere sergeant!"

13

The Valley Campaign

No one saw the danger of McClellan's attack on Richmond clearer than General Robert E. Lee. The Army of the Potomac outnumbered the Confederate forces probably two to one. Here the military genius of General Lee became prominent.

He sent General Stonewall Jackson into the Shenandoah Valley, leading a relatively small army of no more than 4,500 troops. Facing him was Major General Banks with more than 20,000 men, and another army almost as large stood ready in West Virginia. The Union plan was for General Banks to chase Jackson's small force out of the Valley—but it did not work.

Instead, Stonewall Jackson attacked and routed General Banks's large army. This was enough to alert President Lincoln, who sat helplessly at his desk in Washington. He had planned to send Banks and other forces to reinforce General McClellan. Instead, now he pulled them back to ring Washington with more powerful defenses.

Thus, instead of coming to battle having an overwhelming force, the cautious McClellan found himself stripped of many troops. This caused him to stop and think.

Jeff and Tom knew little or nothing of all this. Jackson told no one his plans. He once said that if his coat had the secret plan of battle he would burn it. Now he had simply marched his troops out of

Richmond into the Shenandoah Valley and begun a campaign in which he was to rout and defeat not one but three separate armies.

Jeff wiped his face on his sleeve and glanced over at Charlie Bowers. The smaller boy's face was marked with fatigue for they had marched many hours.

"Let me carry your drum awhile, Charlie, and your gear," Jeff said. The smaller boy protested, but Jeff shook him off. "I'm not real tired yet. Give me them things." He hooked the drum around his neck, grabbed Charlie's knapsack, and said, "Come on, we've got to keep up."

Charlie huffed and puffed. The dust from the feet of thousands of marching men had coated his face and that of every other soldier in the army.

"I wish Stonewall would make up his mind," he gasped. "He's gonna walk our legs off before this is over."

Jeff was ready to drop himself. He had seen older soldiers fall out, simply unable to keep pace, but he had determined not to show his weariness. "I reckon he's got to do it. They've got so many more men than we have that we have to keep moving around so they won't get us penned up."

Curly Henson was walking behind the two boys. He also was red-faced, and veins stood out on his forehead. "Well," he growled, "I didn't know you'd become a strategist, Jeff. Maybe Stonewall and General Lee ought to let you in on their war planning."

Jeff turned and grinned back at the big man. He had learned to like the huge fellow, even though he had not at first. "Oh, if they get into real trouble I expect they'll call me in, Curly." He noticed the man's flushed face. "I still got plenty of water left —you need a drink?"

Curly had drunk his own canteen empty an hour ago. His lips were cracked, but he said, "Oh, I wouldn't want to take your water."

"I'm not thirsty. You take it. We'll be coming to a creek soon."

Curly took the wooden canteen from Jeff and drank several swallows. Wiping his lips on his sleeve, he put the cap on and handed it back. "That was good," he said. "Thanks a lot, youngster." He looked down at his huge body and shook his head. "Takes more to move what I got than what you got, I guess. I'm about ready to drop, to tell the truth."

Murmurs went up and down from the soldiers on both sides. At that moment there was a commotion, and somebody said, "There comes Stonewall," and immediately they all turned to look.

General Jackson rode up on the horse he called Sorrel. His cap was down over his face, and his mind seemed to be a thousand miles away. The troops put up a little cheer for him, but he didn't even seem to hear them.

"He's not very friendly, is he?" Curly Henson said.

"He is too!" Charlie Bowers disagreed. "He talked to me that night at the camp meeting just like he was a common soldier—told me about the Lord and all."

"Well, I don't think he's thinking about the Lord today—he's thinking about Yankees," Sergeant Mapes said. He was striding along, looking ahead, his long legs covering ground faster than anyone else. "I think we're going to run into something pretty soon. When Stonewall looks like that, there's usually trouble brewing."

Two hours later they did exactly that. Jeff sensed a battle was coming when he heard the crackle of musket fire far ahead.

"That's it," Sergeant Lafe Simms groaned. "We're in for it now."

Jeff moved over beside Lafe. "You be careful now. Mathilda wouldn't like it if anything happened to you. Neither would Jake or Aileen."

He had met the burly Sergeant Simms when he took Esther to Kentucky on the train. He had been surprised to see him in Stonewall's regiment.

Sergeant Simms gave him a brief grin. "She told me to tell you the same thing in her last letter, Jeff. Keep your head down—we're going to see the elephant today for sure."

"What do you mean 'see the elephant'?"

"Aw, that's what they call seeing a battle. Don't know why."

The rifle fire became louder and louder, and soon Lieutenant Potter came running back with Tom at his side.

"Sergeant, get the men in battle line. We've struck an outfit up there—General Fremont's troops. We've got to crush their flank."

Tom began calling out loudly as did the other sergeants. Soon the troops were in a battle line and were advancing over a broken field.

Then a tremendous crash almost deafened Jeff. He looked back and saw that some men were down from an exploded shell. Some were still moving in the dust, and others were lying still.

Fear ran along Jeff's spine, but then Lieutenant Potter came along. "Be ready, Jeff. When we have to right flank or left flank the boys, you sound out loud and clear. Remember what the signal for charge is. Stonewall will charge us as sure as the world."

After that the air was filled with smoke and sound and whistling bullets. Jeff remembered once that George Washington had said the sound of bullets had a pleasing sound, but he didn't think so. They whined around like bees, and he had to stop thinking of it.

Finally Sergeant Potter got his orders from a courier and yelled, "Sound the charge, Jeff!"

Jeff began rattling out the charge. The men rammed balls in their muskets and moved forward. They were spread out in three lines about ten feet apart. Ahead Jeff could see muskets winking as they exploded, and he was tempted to lie down.

He suddenly was aware that Tom was beside him. Tom's face was already black with gunpowder from firing his musket. "Take care now," Tom said. "You stay back when the attack begins."

Jeff didn't say anything, but he determined to go with the men.

Then, as they charged against a broken field, he saw blue uniforms ahead. The Confederates were yelling at the top of their lungs. They had heard that the Rebel yell frightened the Yankees, so they screamed until they had no breath left.

The battle went on for some time. Sometimes the Confederates charged, sometimes they backed away when the opposing force got too strong. At last General Jackson rode along the line shouting, "We've got 'em! We've got 'em! Lieutenant Potter! Charge that gun emplacement over there! Put that cannon out of action!"

"Yes, sir!" Potter yelled. "Sergeant Carter, take a squad, flank that cannon, and put it out."

"Yes, sir!" Tom called out the names of a half dozen men. They left, running low to the ground, and disappeared into a grove of trees.

Jeff had fallen back with the rest of the waiting troops. Several men were down, and he went around giving them water, but he worried about Tom.

One of his friends—Phineas Rollins, a tall, raw-boned man—was lying down, holding his stomach. Jeff took one look, and his heart sank. Wounds like that were almost always fatal. He said, "Can I get you anything, Phineas?"

Phineas looked up and gasped. "No, I reckon I won't need anything—but you might say a prayer for me, Jeff."

Jeff knelt down beside the tall man. "Does it hurt much?"

"No, not really." Phineas looked down at his stomach and shook his head. "It'll be a miracle if I live through this. Write to my wife, will you? Tell her I died talking about her."

"Don't talk like that Phineas," Jeff cried. "God can help us. Let's pray." So Jeff began to pray in a halting, stumbling way. He had never prayed for a man like this, but he poured his heart out. When he finally said, "In Jesus' Name, save this man's life. Amen," he looked at his friend. "I'll get a stretcher bearer, Phineas. We'll get you to the hospital, to the doctors."

He ran until he found the ambulance where the surgeon was already at work at the field hospital. He saw two stretcher bearers standing idle and persuaded them to go with him. They made their way back, and soon Phineas was on his way to a field hospital.

Jeff took a deep breath and began hunting for Tom. He began to grow fearful and started to ask everyone. But no one had seen his brother since the last action started.

And then he heard someone call his name. "Jeff! Oh, Jeff!"

With relief he saw that it was Tom. He ran to him and noticed that Tom was holding his left hand, which was wrapped in some kind of white cloth. "Tom! Are you all right?"

"Well, I got a little nick in my hand here." He held up the bloody bandage. "Not bad—but I can't handle a musket."

At that moment Lieutenant Potter came by. He saw Tom and asked, "How bad is it, Sergeant?"

"Oh, it'll be all right." Tom drew the cloth back and showed the wound. "Going to take a while before I can load a musket, I guess."

Potter shook his head. "Just the luck. Well, are you able to take a detail? We got some Yankee prisoners here. Got to get 'em back to Richmond."

"Yes, sir. I'll do that." He looked at Jeff and said, "If it's all right, I'd like to take Jeff here with me."

Potter considered, then said, "Yes, take the boy with you."

Jeff and Tom got their gear and met the party of some twenty Federal prisoners. There was a wagon carrying some wounded men, and they were to take them too.

"Well, at least we get to ride back," Tom said. "You'll have to drive." They climbed up on the wagon seat. Jeff said, "Giddup," and the team

133

surged forward. Two guards followed along behind the prisoners.

Jeff said, "Phineas got shot in the stomach. We've got him in the wagon here. You think he'll be all right, Tom? I sure pray he will."

Tom too knew that most men shot in the stomach did not live, but he said, "You know what Pa always said—God can do anything."

"I guess I'll just believe that then." Jeff hesitated. "Still pretty hard to believe God's gonna get Pa out of that prison. Me and Leah's trying to believe it though. I think she believes it more than I do."

Tom held his wounded hand against his chest to avoid the jolting of the wagon. "You listen to that girl," he said, fatigue in his voice. "She's got more gumption and more sense than most men I've known."

14

Under Arrest

The three large pecan trees in back of Silas Carter's house dropped their leaves annually and made a thick carpet. Next to the house and behind the tool-shed they were simply raked up to make a path. Leah had found that these moldy piles were prime hunting grounds for night crawlers. The huge worms that could almost wiggle away when the leaves were raked back made excellent bait. Leah had kept the household well supplied with thumping bream, bass, and blue channel catfish.

Late in May she was out with a bucket, capturing some of the lively creatures for a good afternoon's fishing trip. She reached under the thick mattress of leaves, threw it away, and there saw at least a dozen night crawlers, some seven or eight inches long, scrambling wildly away from the light.

Quickly she made a grab and seized four of them before the rest disappeared under the leaves. "Gotcha," she said with satisfaction. She tossed a handful of moldy leaves into the bucket to cover the squirming bait and proceeded to uncover more.

This was a job she liked. She thought about Jeff's teasing her, for at first she could not stand even to touch a worm, much less thread one on a hook! But a sense of pride came to her as she thought of how she had beaten him on their last fishing trip together.

She had learned to love this backyard. It was enclosed with a high board fence turned gray with age. The yard gave her a sense of being on an island, for the trees grew wildly here. One huge fig tree promised juicy fruit in case she was there to get it in the fall. A weeping willow spread its limbs to the ground. She loved to make whips out of its branches and pretend she was driving a horse and carriage. On a walnut tree she found large balls from last year and delighted in cracking them and picking out the nuts with the blade of a sharp knife. She had made a walnut cake three days earlier, and Uncle Silas had pronounced it the best ever made.

"I wish Jeff were here and that he didn't have to go to that old war," she muttered, scooping up another worm and tossing it into the bucket.

Every time she thought of him or Tom or Royal, sadness came over her. The war was so terrible. She knew that all over the country mothers were hearing about their sons being killed, wives about their husbands, and children about their fathers.

Depressed, she sat down, her back to the toolhouse. She was thinking about home and Morena and how baby Esther was doing when suddenly voices caught her attention. She heard the gate close and then Sarah's voice.

"Come back here if you have to talk, Wesley—I don't want to disturb Uncle Silas."

Leah started to get up and let them know she was there, but when she half rose she heard the captain's voice, and something in it made her sit back down. She thought she shouldn't interrupt. Then through the willow branches she could see them.

"Sarah, I think you've tormented me quite long enough," Wesley Lyons said. There was almost a whine in his voice, and yet he was angry too, Leah could tell.

"I haven't tormented you at all." Sarah's voice was calm, but Leah knew her sister well enough to know that she was disturbed. "If there's any tormenting being done, I'm on the receiving end of it."

"I don't think I have ever been accused of tormenting a young lady. As a matter of fact, my attentions have always been welcomed in that quarter."

"I'm sure they have, Wesley, and I appreciate the attention you've shown to me, but—"

"Well, you certainly don't act like it! I've spent days just trying to get you to be civil, Sarah, and I don't see why you have to be so standoffish. What is it in me that you find objectionable?"

"Oh, Wes, nothing that . . ." Sarah found several things objectionable about Captain Wesley Lyons, but she was too weary of the argument to carry it on. "It's just that I'll only be here for a limited time. I'll go back to Kentucky, and you won't see me anymore. Wesley, why don't you go find some nice young lady, one of these that will welcome your attention, as you say? You're wasting your time on me."

The captain stared at her, then said, "I suppose it's that sergeant that you're interested in."

"We've been friends a long time. We grew up together. Of course we're friends."

"Don't try to tell me that! You're in love with him, aren't you?"

Sarah suddenly looked directly at him. "Yes," she said rather loudly. Her eyes were sparkling, and the anger that she had kept down suddenly flared. "I'm in love with him, and if this war ever ends and we both live through it, I expect to marry him one day. Now will you leave me alone!"

"Yes, I certainly will!" Lyons jammed his cap on, turned, and strode stiff-legged toward the gate.

Leah heard it slam, and then she heard Sarah begin to cry. She wanted to comfort her, but she didn't want her sister to know that she had been an eavesdropper. Finally, Sarah seemed to get control of herself. Leah heard the screen door close.

With her fists clenched, she struck the ground and whispered, "I wish that old captain would go away and never come back!"

* * *

"Your name is Sarah Carter?"

A lieutenant was standing at the door, a piece of paper in his hand. Sarah had never seen him before, and for one moment she thought he had come to tell her something had happened to Tom or Jeff. "Yes—I'm Sarah Carter. Is something wrong?"

The officer seemed a little embarrassed. "My name is Phelps, miss, Lieutenant Phelps. I'm afraid I'll have to ask you to come with me."

Sarah looked past Lieutenant Phelps and saw two soldiers, privates, armed with muskets. They were watching her curiously.

She turned back to the lieutenant. "Go with you? Why, go where? Whatever for?"

"I have to inform you," Lieutenant Phelps said, "that you are under arrest."

Leah had been standing inside the screen door, and now she came bursting out. "Under *arrest?* You can't arrest my sister!"

138

Sarah reached over and held Leah's shoulder. The shock had stilled her for a moment, but she gathered herself and said, "Under arrest on what charge?"

"Suspicion of treason. I'm sorry, miss, you'll have to come with me right now."

Sarah felt Leah's body trembling under her hand, and thoughts ran through her mind. Finally she said, "I suppose these charges began with Captain Wesley Lyons?"

Lieutenant Phelps lowered his eyes. Then he shook his head. "I'm afraid I can't give you any information, ma'am. You'll have a chance to defend yourself and ask any questions. Please, could you come with me now?"

"Am I allowed to get a change of clothes? How long will I be held?"

"Well, of course, go right ahead, ma'am. I think I'd take some clothes, if I were you." He hesitated, then said, "These things usually take a while."

"Very well."

Sarah turned and went into the house.

Leah followed her. "What in the world is it? Why would they be arresting you?"

"I had a fight with Captain Lyons. I expect this is his way of getting back. I'll have to go explain this to Uncle Silas."

Silas was sitting in his wheelchair, and when Sarah had finished, he said, "Nonsense! As errant nonsense as I ever heard! We'll get to the bottom of this."

He started to wheel himself forward, but Sarah said, "It will do no good. The lieutenant is determined."

"Well, I'll try anyway. Wheel me out there, Leah."

Leah wheeled Uncle Silas out to the front porch where he argued loudly with Lieutenant Phelps, but in the end it did no good.

Then Sarah came down the stairs wearing a light cloak and carrying a small canvas suitcase. She leaned over and kissed Uncle Silas. "I'll have to go. Take care of Leah, Uncle Silas."

The old man and Leah watched silently as Sarah was escorted into an ambulance that was used for transporting prisoners. When the vehicle had moved out of sight, Leah said, "We've got to do something, Uncle Silas."

"Wheel me back inside, girl. Time for me to start writing letters, and then you'll have to see that they get delivered. I'm writing Jeff Davis himself about this."

* * *

Tom and Jeff walked down Elm Street. At the sight of the familiar house, Tom said, "I'll sure be glad to see Sarah and Leah and their Uncle Silas too." His arm was in a sling, but he had been told the wound was not serious. He grinned at Jeff. "I guess it's worth a little shot in the hand to get to come back for a while—but I feel a little guilty."

"So do I," Jeff answered. "You've got a reason for not being in the battle, but I don't."

"Well, from what I hear, Stonewall's eating the lunch of those Federals," Tom remarked with pleasure. "I hear he's got two or three generals, and their whole army's running around like dogs after their own tail. That Stonewall, he's some general."

They walked up onto the porch and knocked, and Jeff was almost bowled over when the screen door swung outward and struck him. "Hey! Watch out, Leah!" he complained. "I know you're glad to see me, but—"

"Oh, Jeff! Tom! They've arrested Sarah!"

Tom flinched as though she had struck him. "Arrested *Sarah? Who* arrested her?" Tom demanded.

"Somebody from the War Department. It's all that old Captain Lyons's fault!"

"What happened? Tell me about it," Tom pressed.

They stood on the porch while Leah told the story. She even included how she had unintentionally eavesdropped. "I could tell he was mad as hops. Then that same day, a lieutenant came and took Sarah away."

Jeff shook his head. "Why, that's the craziest thing I ever heard of—Sarah, a spy!"

Leah frowned worriedly. "I know it's crazy, but there's all kinds of crazy stories going around Richmond. There *are* some Federal spies here—everybody knows that. And there are Southern spies in Washington—like Mrs. Greenhow I told you about. People are turning up 'spies' everywhere. Most of them aren't, of course, but they just go around and arrest people and hold them in jail. They won't even let them see a lawyer."

"What's being done? What have *you* done? What has Uncle Silas done?" Tom asked rapidly.

"Well, he's written letters to almost everybody —the secretary of war and President Davis himself," Leah said. "But I guess they're pretty busy. We haven't heard back from anybody yet, and I'm afraid Uncle Silas is going to pop his cork if something doesn't happen soon. He's so mad he can't even talk straight."

They found this to be true. When Tom and Jeff went into the old man's bedroom, they found him seated in a chair and waving a cane. At once he began ranting and raving about the idiots that ran the Confederacy and tried his best to get Tom to shove him down to the War Department.

"I'll face Jeff Davis face to face, man to man!" he sputtered. "If he lets this kind of thing go on, he's no man for the presidency of the Southern Confederacy."

"Now take it easy, Uncle Silas," Tom said. He summoned up a smile. "I'm afraid you'd shoot him if I took you down there. Let me go see what I can do. I know one of the lieutenants who works in the War Department. He was in our outfit till he got shot in the foot—they put him there to work at a desk job. Let me see what I can do."

Tom left at once, refusing to let Jeff go with him.

After he had gone, Jeff and Leah talked for an hour, mostly about Sarah. Finally Leah said almost tearfully, "Well, we were only worried about your dad—now it looks like my family is in about as bad a shape as yours." Her lips trembled.

Jeff patted her shoulder awkwardly. "Don't forget now what you made me agree to. We were going to trust the Lord to take care of my father. Why can't we do the same thing for Sarah?"

"Will you pray with me, Jeff? I'm really scared," Leah said. "I couldn't bear it if anything happened to her."

"Why, sure. I guess I'm going to have to learn to be more of a praying fellow," Jeff said. "Looks like things we can't handle keep piling up on us."

The two bowed their heads, and they prayed for Sarah. Then they prayed for Jeff's father.

When they were through, Leah said softly, "Thank you, Jeff. It's nice to have somebody to pray with."

"Sure is."

* * *

Tom Majors was a level-headed young man. He kept calm for two days, but he was unable to get in to see Sarah. Furthermore, he was unable to find anyone who would even talk about the problem. The friend he had depended on said simply, "Well, that's how it is, Tom. I guess you better write a letter to the secretary of war or somebody."

"That's already been done," Tom said, "and it didn't do a bit of good." He left the office angrily. Perhaps things would have been all right, but he walked the streets of Richmond letting the anger build up in him.

"Captain Wesley Lyons—he's behind all this!" he muttered to himself. He clenched his teeth and nodded. "All right, we'll just see what Captain Wesley Lyons has to say."

He went to the building that housed the Quartermaster Corps, marched inside, and faced the corporal in an outer office. "I'm here to see Captain Lyons."

"What's your name, Sergeant?"

"I'm Sergeant Tom Majors, and you might as well tell him I'll sit here in this office till doomsday, so he might as well see me."

The clerk looked startled, then grinned. "I'll tell him," he said.

He disappeared into an inner office. There was the sound of voices, and then the door opened. "He says he won't see you. Sorry about that, Sergeant Majors."

Tom surged forward and brushed the corporal aside.

"Hey! You can't go in there!" the corporal protested, but Tom slammed the door in his face.

Inside the office Captain Wesley Lyons blinked in surprise, then came to his feet. "Get out of my office, Majors. I told you I wouldn't see you."

"Well, you do see me, don't you?" Tom said. "I'm standing right in front of you, Captain."

"You—you're disobeying a direct order," Lyons shouted. "Now get out of here!"

"I'll leave when you tell me why you've had Sarah Carter arrested. You know she's no spy!"

Lyons came around from behind his desk. He was taller than Tom, and he was angry. "I'm giving you one last chance. Get out of this office, or I'll have you arrested for insubordination!"

Tom ordinarily would have obeyed, but anger had built up in him for too long. "I'm not leaving until you tell me what you did—or let *me* tell *you* what you did. You couldn't win Sarah for yourself so you had her put in jail. What kind of a man do you call yourself anyhow? You're not a man—you're a spoiled brat!"

"Corporal! Corporal!" Lyons bawled. He reached out to turn Tom around and shove him out the door. Just as the door opened and the corporal entered, Tom pushed Lyons backward.

"Did you see that? He struck me! Place this man under arrest, Corporal!" The corporal looked startled and said, "But, sir—"

"Did you hear me? Did you hear that order? I said, place this man under arrest!"

The corporal blinked. "I'm sorry, Sergeant. You see how it is. You'll have to come with me."

Tom wanted to throw himself on Lyons and batter him with both fists. Fortunately he regained some of his calm, took a deep breath, slowly expelled it. "Yes, sir. I'll obey your order."

"You needn't think being mild and meek will help you now. You'll be shot for this. Now get him out of here."

When they were outside, the corporal looked at him curiously. "Well, you sure stirred him up. What did you say to him?"

"It was about a friend of mine he had arrested." He saw a light flicker in the corporal's eyes. "I see you know about it."

"Well, I know a little, but I can't talk about it."

Tom saw that the man knew considerably more than he was saying. "All right, let's go get me put in jail," he said. "Do me one favor. Miss Carter has an elderly uncle named Silas Carter. He lives on Elm Street where she was arrested. Would you send word down there what's happened to me? And you might send word to my unit too."

"What's your unit?"

"I'm in the Stonewall Brigade"

"You work for Stonewall Jackson?" The corporal whistled. "I wish I did. He's eating those Yankees alive out in the Valley." He looked at Tom's bandaged hand. "You get shot fighting with Stone-wall?"

"Yes, that's why I'm here."

"Well, that ought to help you some. Stonewall's really somebody right now!"

15

A Brief Trial
and a Quick Verdict

Mrs. Mary Chesnut was accustomed to receiving guests. Her home was the center for the highest society of Richmond. General Lee, General Hood, and President Davis were frequent guests. Mrs. Chesnut's best friend was Varina Davis, the wife of the president.

But when she opened the door early one morning, after hearing an insistent knock, she was taken aback by the sight of a young girl, staring at her with tragic eyes.

"Mrs. Chesnut," the girl said, "I guess you don't remember me."

"Why, I'm afraid I don't, child."

"My sister and I were at a tea that you had. I'm Leah Carter, and my sister's name is Sarah."

"Why, yes, of course, I remember you now. Come in, come in at once." Mary Chesnut stepped back, and Leah entered. "How is your uncle? He was very ill, if I remember correctly."

"He's fine, Mrs. Chesnut. But it's my sister— she's in awful trouble."

Mary Chesnut stared at the girl. "Well, perhaps you'd better come into the parlor. We can talk about it there." She led the way down the hall. Opening a door, she took Leah inside a room that was rather small and filled with sewing baskets and fragments of quilts in various stages. "Sit down right there. Move that quilt out of the way, Leah," Mrs. Chesnut said. "Now then, tell me all about it."

Leah hesitated. "It's so awful. You remember that there was a captain who was attentive to my sister."

"Why, yes, I do remember. Captain Lyons, wasn't it?"

"That's him. Well, he's been coming to call on her ever since that tea."

"I suppose your sister is very flattered to have such a handsome, eligible young man calling on her."

"Oh, no, ma'am, she doesn't want him, and that's what caused the trouble."

Mrs. Chesnut blinked. She saw that the girl's lower lip was trembling as if she were on the verge of tears. "What is it, child?" she asked. "What's wrong with your sister?"

"She's been arrested!" Leah burst out, and then tears did run down her cheeks. She let them flow unheeded and said, "She's no spy, Mrs. Chesnut. She wouldn't do anything like that. We just came here to take care of my Uncle Silas."

"Now, dry those tears." Mrs. Chesnut produced a silk handkerchief and handed it to her. "Tell me all about it. Go very slowly now." She sat and listened until the story had poured out of Leah. Then Mrs. Chesnut said, "Why, it sounds frightful. When is the trial to be?"

"I think it's today, but they won't tell us anything. They won't let us in to see her either."

Mary Chesnut was a woman of firm convictions. She was a little on the rebellious side, refusing to accept the traditional role of a woman. She had, at times, a rather sharp tongue. Somehow the sight of Leah's tearful face angered her. She said, "Let me get my cape. We'll go down and find my husband, Colonel Chesnut. Then we'll see about this!"

Things happened rapidly. Leah was bundled into a carriage, and all the way to the War Department she found herself telling the lady beside her about life in Kentucky. By the time they had reached the War Department and were out of the carriage, Mary Chesnut knew all about Jeff and Tom and their father, Nelson Majors.

Mrs. Chesnut said, "Come along. We'll have to explain all of this to my husband. I'm sure he'll be able to help."

They found Colonel Chesnut, who was one of Jefferson Davis's advisers, with an office full of people. His wife simply brushed them aside, shooed them out of the office, and said, "Now, husband, you sit down and listen to this young lady."

The colonel was a distinguished-looking man, rather slight. He was accustomed to his wife's abrupt ways. "Very well, my dear," he said. "I suppose it must be important."

"It certainly is! Just listen!"

Twenty minutes later Colonel Chesnut had the whole story. He had not said a word. But as soon as Leah was finished, he said, "I hadn't heard about this. You two wait right here while I go and do some checking."

As soon as he was out of the room, Mary Chesnut went over and put her arm around Leah. "Don't you worry now. My husband may be a little slow at times, but when he gets that look in his eye, I know there's going to be action. It's rather strange, that look. He looks like he's just decided to lower his head and ram it through a brick wall! A stubborn man, but very sweet."

Colonel Chesnut was gone for almost thirty minutes. When he came back he was bustling. "Come along," he said. He belted on a saber, jammed a soft felt Confederate hat on his head, and said, "I think we'll attend your sister's trial, Miss Leah."

He led them across the yard toward a large, red brick building, where a soldier saluted him sharply. Then he conducted them to a pair of large double doors guarded by two privates. "Is the trial going on?"

"Yes, sir," one of the men said. "It just started. Do you want to go in, Colonel?"

"Yes, and these are my guests."

"Yes, sir." He opened the doors wide, and Colonel Chesnut marched in. His wife clutched one arm and Leah the other.

Leah was scared when she saw six officers seated at a table. Across from them was her sister, and she wanted to cry out, but Mrs. Chesnut squeezed her arm.

"It'll be all right, dear. Let my husband handle it."

"Why, Colonel Chesnut," another colonel said, looking up with surprise. "I didn't expect you here, sir."

Colonel Chesnut turned to his wife. "You sit here, dear. Leah, you sit down with us." Then he looked across the room to where Captain Wesley Lyons sat with a startled look in his eye.

"You have an interest in this case, Colonel?"

"Yes, I do. Proceed, and I will let my feelings be known at the proper time."

"Why—why, of course, Colonel Chesnut."

The officer in charge seemed flustered, but he quickly pulled himself together. "Now then, we will hear the evidence against the accused."

A small, rotund man sitting at a table to one side rose and cast one look at Colonel Chesnut. He cleared his throat. "The accused has been brought to this place on charges of treason."

He rambled on for quite a while, and finally the presiding officer said with some irritation, "We have many cases to hear, Captain. What is the evidence against Miss Carter?"

"Letters, sir. I have them right here." He opened one and began to read. It was a simple enough letter. Leah remembered when Sarah had written it. It simply gave a brief account of what they were doing with their time and reported on Uncle Silas's condition. It did mention that there was a great deal of activity and that McClellan's army was expected to move at any time. It was the kind of talk that people made every day.

When the prosecuting attorney had read the letter, the colonel in charge said, "Where is the proof of treason?"

"You must see it, Colonel! She's telling this man—her father, who is an agent for the North—about our troops, about what's happening here in Richmond."

A young man seated beside Sarah said, "I object, sir." He stood to his feet. "There's nothing in that letter that isn't known to everybody in the North. We all know that McClellan is on his way. There's no military secret there."

"Objection sustained! We'd better hear the rest of those letters, sir," the colonel said, and his face grew stern. "And we'd better hear something more incriminating than that, or we will find someone in contempt for wasting the time of the court."

"Why—why, yes, sir!" The prosecutor wiped his forehead. He read through several letters.

Finally the presiding officer said, "Is this the sum of your evidence?"

"Sir, her father is an agent for the North!"

The colonel looked across at Sarah. "Is this true, Miss Carter?"

"My father is not an agent for the North. He is a sutler," Sarah said calmly. "He sells supplies to the troops just as your sutlers do. In addition to that, he passes out Bibles and tracts. You can confirm this very easily."

The colonel's face grew red as he stared at the prosecuting attorney. "This is the extent of your evidence?" he repeated.

"Well . . . yes, sir."

"Who had this woman arrested?'

"Why, I believe Captain Lyons brought the matter to our attention." The prosecuting attorney gave the captain an angry look. Leah saw he was upset at being put in such an embarrassing position. "Perhaps he may have more evidence than he's given me."

Colonel Ames, the head of the court, said, "Captain, you may speak. Why have you brought these charges on this flimsy evidence?"

Captain Lyons was accustomed to being in charge of things, but the eyes of all six men were fixed on him. He glanced at Colonel Chesnut. "Why, I thought it my duty to bring the matter to the court's attention." That must have sounded feeble even to his own ears.

Colonel Ames stared at him, then looked across the room at Sarah. "We will keep this on an informal basis, I think. Miss Carter, can you think of any reason why Captain Lyons would accuse you of spying for the Union?"

Sarah said without hesitation, "He has been trying to court me. When I expressed a preference for a sergeant in General Stonewall's brigade, he became very angry. I can only assume that this is the cause of his accusations."

A silence fell over the room. Colonel Ames looked at Colonel Chesnut. Some message seemed to pass between the two men. Colonel Ames said loudly, "I declare this case dismissed. Miss Carter, we must ask your forgiveness for the unjust accusations." Then his head turned. "Captain Lyons, you will remain. The court has a few words to say to you."

The defense attorney said, "Thank you, Colonel Ames." He reached down and shook Sarah's hand.

She rose and stood before the court. "Thank you, Colonel Ames and all you gentlemen," she said. Then she turned, and Leah met her, throwing her arms around her.

"Come along—we'll go now," Mrs. Chesnut said.

The four of them left, and when they were outside, Sarah turned to Mary Chesnut and to her husband. "I can't thank you both enough for—"

"Oh—" Colonel Chesnut waved his hand in a gesture of disdain "—it would have come to nothing anyway. That fool of a captain should have known better. I hope they put him in the stockade for being an idiot."

"Will you come back to the house with us?" Mrs. Chesnut asked.

"I really need to get home," Sarah said, "but we'll call later to thank you properly."

That should have been the end of it. Sarah went home with Leah, and the two had a little celebration with Uncle Silas. They were singing the praises of the Chesnuts.

However, on the next day a letter came from the colonel:

My dear Miss Carter,

There have been repercussions concerning your case. I, myself, am totally convinced of your innocence and so are the six men on the board. However, it seems that the father of Wesley Lyons is a man of considerable influence. I will not attempt to justify this, but he has brought great pressure to bear. As a result, I am forced to ask that you leave Richmond and return to your home in Kentucky.

Your younger sister, I trust, will be able to care for your uncle. Once again, rest assured I will pursue this, but it will take some time as these things do.

Regretfully yours,
Colonel Chesnut

Sarah looked up blankly when she had read the letter, and Leah cried, "Why, they can't make you go home!"

"I'm afraid they can, Leah. This is their country, and Colonel Chesnut wouldn't have written this if there hadn't been tremendous pressure. I'll have to go."

She would not have to go to the train station alone, however, for Colonel Chesnut had pursued his investigation. He had Tom freed at once, and that young man came flying to Silas Carter's house. Sarah opened the door herself and found herself wrapped in his arms—or in one of them anyhow. The other was still bandaged.

"Are you all right, Sarah?" he asked. "I was so worried about you."

"Oh, yes, I'm fine." She laughed nervously. "But I've got to go back to Kentucky, Tom."

"Colonel Chesnut told me. But it won't be for long. He's working on it, and he'll get you back here soon."

"I hope so. I hate to leave Leah here all alone, but there's no other way it seems."

The next day Sarah said her good-byes to Leah and Uncle Silas, and Tom took her to the station. They stood on the platform as the train huffed and puffed, sending great clouds of steam into the air.

"I hate like fury for you to go!" Tom groaned. "Just doesn't seem right! Seems like we spend our lives saying good-bye."

Sarah had slept little, and her eyes looked forlorn, but she managed to smile. "It won't be forever. I need to go home anyway and help take care of that baby sister of yours. You watch out for Leah."

"I will." Tom hesitated, then put his good arm around her and kissed her. "Good-bye, but it won't be long."

"Take care of yourself," Sarah whispered. "Oh, be careful! Don't let anything happen to you." Then she whirled and boarded the train.

Tom watched it roll out of the station and pick up speed. It grew smaller in the distance and finally disappeared around a curve. He turned and walked slowly away as despondent as he'd ever been in his whole life.

16

A Gift from Heaven

Stonewall Jackson's campaign in the Valley made him a famous man. His soldiers became known as Jackson's "Foot Cavalry." The armies that he had defeated never got to Richmond to help McClellan. Instead they all retreated to Washington—to the shame of their generals.

Then on June 12, 1862, General Jeb Stuart performed a magnificent feat. He led his cavalry in a ride completely around the Union army. When he returned to Richmond, he had the position of all the Federal troops for General Lee. Richmond was buzzing with excitement.

The Stonewall Brigade had been drawn back from the Valley to join the fight to save Richmond. Tom was still recuperating from his hand injury but was able to at least help with his squad. Jeff expected to be called any minute, for it was certain that the battle for Richmond would take place at any time.

On June 15, Jeff came by the Carter house wearing his best uniform. His hair had been freshly cut by one of his fellow soldiers and was slicked back.

When he entered, Leah cried out, "My! Don't you look nice!"

Jeff shrugged. "I guess, if you say so." He saw she had brushed her own hair carefully and wore it a different way. She was wearing a new dress too. It was light blue with dark blue lace at the sleeves and around the bodice. He noted that she was growing up. "You're not a little girl anymore," he said with a grin. "You look real pretty, Leah."

She flushed. "Where have you been for the last two days?" she asked, changing the subject.

"Oh, I went over with Tom to see how everybody was doing. We lost several men in the Valley." He frowned. "The one man I thought we'd lose for sure was Phineas Rawlings—he got shot in the stomach. I was afraid he'd die, but he didn't. We went to the hospital, and he's doing fine."

Then he noticed there was a mysterious air about Leah.

She said, "You know what day today is?"

Jeff grinned. "I guess so. A fellow doesn't have many birthdays in a year. Pretty nice that you and I have the same birthday, isn't it?" He gave her an odd look. "Are you fishing for a birthday present?"

"No!"

"Well, I got you one anyhow." He reached into his pocket and produced a small package wrapped in white paper with a blue ribbon around it. "Here. Hope you like it."

Leah flushed again and took the gift. Her fingers trembled a little as she carefully took off the ribbon and laid it to one side. Then she unfolded the wrapper slowly. Inside was a small box. She took the lid off and stood staring down at its contents. When she looked up her green eyes were enormous. "Oh, Jeff, it's *beautiful!*" she said, drawing out the last word. "Where did you get it?"

"One of the sergeants in the company posted next to ours sold it to me. He'd bought it for his girlfriend, but they broke up, so he let me have it. I think he was glad to get rid of it, because it reminded him of her."

Leah held the box carefully and pulled out a gold locket with a fine gold chain. She laid it reverently in her palm and admired it. "It's the prettiest locket I've ever seen!"

Jeff coughed, embarrassed. When she looked up at him, he said, "Well, open it up!"

"It opens?" Leah carefully inserted her thumbnail in the tiny groove around the oval locket. It opened smoothly. She cried out with delight. "Why, Jeff, it's *you!*"

Jeff felt his face redden. "Aw, some of us had our picture made by one of them picture-making fellows. I just cut mine out and put it in there. You can throw it away if you want to."

"I won't ever do that! Here, help me put it on!" She handed him the locket, turned around, and held up her long, blonde hair.

Jeff reached around her to get the end of the locket. Then for a few moments he struggled to fasten the clasp. "This thing's so tiny my fingers feel like thumbs," he complained. "All right, there it is," he said, stepping back.

"Come on, I want to look in the mirror." She grabbed his hand and pulled him into the parlor where a gold frame held a small looking glass. She admired herself, turning this way and that. "Oh, it's so pretty!" She turned around and impulsively took his hand. "Thank you, Jeff. It's the nicest present I ever got in my whole life!"

His face grew warm, and he mumbled, "Oh, well, I'm glad you like it."

Leah stood looking at him for a moment and said, "I've got you a present too—but you'll have to do what I say."

"Why do I have to do what you say? Just give me the present."

"No, come in here." She led him into the parlor. "Now, you sit down right there." She pushed him toward a leather-covered chair, and he plopped down in it. "Now, shut your eyes."

"Oh, shoot, Leah—this is for babies!" he protested.

"Here, you hold your hands over your eyes, and don't you peek." She took his hands and put them over his face. He mumbled another protest, but she said, "If you don't mind me, I won't give you a present—and no cake either."

"Well, all right," Jeff said. "Let me have it then."

"You wait right there, and I'll be right back. And don't you *dare* peek!"

"I won't," Jeff muttered. He heard her footsteps leaving the room. He thought he heard voices, and then he heard her come back. He held out his hand. "All right, let's have it. I hope it's something good to eat."

"It's something better than that!" Leah said, and there was something strange in her voice.

Suddenly Jeff felt a hand on his head, and he straightened up abruptly, startled by the touch.

"You can look now," Leah said.

Jeff lowered his hands, looked up, and shock ran through him.

"Hello, Son. Happy birthday."

"Pa!" Jeff leaped out of his chair, threw his arms around his father, and hugged him tight.

Lieutenant Majors said, "Now, don't break every bone I've got, boy."

Jeff could not think clearly. He took a step back and said, "Pa, I can't believe it! How did you get here? How long have you been here? Where—"

Nelson Majors held up a hand. He was pale, but his eyes were clear, and he had gained some weight. "I just got in yesterday. I wanted to find you right away, but Leah said wait till today and it would be a birthday present you'd never forget."

"Boy, that's right!" He was suddenly close to tears for some reason he could not explain. A lump rose in his throat, and he could not have said another word if his life had depended on it.

Suddenly Leah came over and kissed him on the cheek. "There! There's your happy birthday present. Isn't it wonderful? Just what we prayed for!"

His father grabbed the two of them and squeezed their shoulders. He was getting his strength back, Jeff saw.

"General Jackson arranged for the exchange," he said. "I got a note from him. He said he'd been praying about it and he knew that others were praying too. So he expected God to make the exchange possible—which He did."

For the next few hours the three could not talk fast enough. Finally Lieutenant Majors said, "Well, God be thanked, I'm back. I wish your mother was here to see this—and I wish Esther was here so that I could see her. But I'm not complaining.

"Happy birthday to both of you. Leah—fourteen years old now, a young woman. I remember you when you were nothing but a rug rat crawling along the carpet, chasing around after Jeff. And you, Jeff—fifteen, almost a man." He looked at them

161

fondly. "That's a strange age, fourteen, fifteen. No longer a child, not yet a man or a woman, but with some of both of it in you. I'm mighty proud of you two, both of you."

He turned abruptly and left the room, saying, "I've got to go visit some more with Uncle Silas. We'll have your birthday cake later, I take it?"

They did have birthday cake. Uncle Silas's cheeks were red, and he looked 100 percent better than he had when Leah had first come. "Best thing that ever happened to me," he declared. "That's some youngun' you got there, Nelson—and that other one too."

After the cake, Jeff and Leah walked out of the house and got their fishing poles. Jeff said, "Can't think of any way to celebrate a birthday better than to go fishing. This time I'm going to show you how to catch fish."

"We'll see about that!" Leah retorted.

They made their way down to the James River again. They talked more than they fished. Even when Jeff lost a large bass when he had it almost to shore, he just laughed and said, "Go on, get bigger. I'll catch you later."

That made Leah think of Old Napoleon. "Napoleon's a year older now than he was when you put him back. We'll go back and catch him someday, won't we, Jeff?"

They stopped fishing and stood on the high bank together, watching the water flow by. Then Jeff said, "You know, I've learned how to trust God more. You've helped me with that, Leah. Something kept telling me to keep on praying, keep on hoping, even when things looked hopeless."

162

"I'm glad," Leah said simply.

The wind was coming off the river, ruffling her fine, blonde hair. They stood for a long time, thinking and talking about other, happier days.

"More bad times are coming," Leah said, "but we'll always be best friends, won't we, Jeff?"

Jeff nodded. "Yes." He thought about that for a moment. "Even when I get married, we'll be best friends."

Leah gave him a sudden glance and was silent. Then she shook her head. "Your wife won't like that."

"She'll have to do what I tell her," Jeff said airily.

"Your wife will have a terrible time," Leah said.

He gave her a condescending grin. "Women aren't able to take care of themselves. They need a man. Let's go."

Turning, he stepped on a patch of slick, red mud. "Hey!" he yelled as his feet flew out from under him. He made a wild grab at Leah but missed and suddenly slid over the bank. He hit the water with a tremendous splash and came up sputtering.

Leah fell to laughing helplessly. "That was wonderful. I never saw such a graceful dive in all my life."

Jeff spit out a mouthful of muddy water and glared up at her. He waded to the bank, but the red mud was hard and slick, and he fell back again almost as violently as the first time.

"Well, don't just stand there. Get a stick!" he yelled.

"Oh, Jeff," Leah said, bending over, "tell me again how helpless women are and how strong all of you men are!"

"Leah, you help me get out of here, you hear?" Jeff said. He stared at her as she continued to laugh. Finally he said, "Please, Leah, give me a hand, will you? I just can't get out by myself."

Leah stopped laughing. "Oh, all right, Jeff, I didn't mean to make fun of you." She reached down to take his hand—and suddenly he grabbed her by the wrist and pulled her straight down. "Jeff! *Jeff!* Don't—" She hit the water headfirst, and it closed around her head.

She came up sputtering and spitting. "My new dress—it's ruined!" she wailed.

It was Jeff's turn to laugh.

The two stood there in the river, Jeff laughing and Leah beating at him with her hands. At last she looked down at the dress, and the humor of the situation struck her. She began to laugh. "Happy birthday, Jeff."

He went a little farther upstream and scrambled up the bank, then reached down and pulled her up. They were muddy from head to foot, and he suddenly gave her a big hug. "Happy birthday, Leah."

"Always best friends?" she asked. Water ran down her hair, dripped off her face. Mud covered the front of her dress.

Jeff looked at her and grinned. "Yes," he said, "best muddy friends in the whole world!"

Get swept away in the many Gilbert Morris adventures from Moody

Kerrigan Kids #1

The Kerrigan Kids are headed to Africa to take pictures and write a story on a once fierce tribe. The Kids may be able to travel to Africa but if Duffy can't learn to swallow her pride and appreciate others, they may be left behind with their dreaded Aunt Minnie!
ISBN#0-8024-1578-4

Kerrigan Kids #2

With a whole countryful of places to explore and exciting new adventures to be had, the Kerrigan Kids can't help but have a good time in England. The Kerrigan Kids also learn an important lesson about having a good attitude and about being a good friend.
ISBN#0-8024-1579-2

Kerrigan Kids #3

After several mishaps including misdirected luggage, the Kerrigans are reminded that bad things can happen to good people and the importance of trusting in God even during difficult circumstances.
ISBN#0-8024-1580-6

Kerrigan Kids #4

The Sunday before they leave, the kids are reminded of the story of the Good Samaritan. When there is no one to meet their two new friends from the plane trip at the airport, the Kerrigan clan puts what they learned about helping other into practice.
ISBN#0-8024-1580-6

Seven Sleepers Series

3681-1   Flight of the Eagles
3682-X   The Gates of Neptune
3683-3   The Swords of Camelot
3684-6   The Caves That Time Forgot
3685-4   Winged Riders of the Desert
3686-2   Empress of the Underworld
3687-0   Voyage of the Dolphin
3691-9   Attack of the Amazons
3692-7   Escape with the Dream Maker
3693-5   The Final Kingdom

Go with Josh and his friends as they are sent by Goel, their spiritual leader, on dangerous and challenging voyages to conquer the forces of darkness in the new world. Ages 10-14

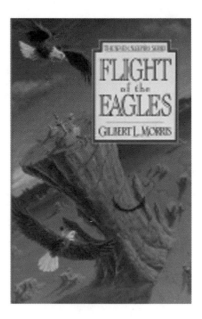

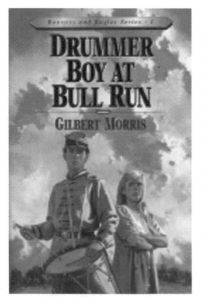

Bonnets and Bugles Series

0911-3   Drummer Boy at Bull Run
0912-1   Yankee Bells in Dixie
0913-X   The Secret of Richmond Manor
0914-8   The Soldier Boy's Discovery
0915-6   Blockade Runner
0916-4   The Gallant Boys of Gettysburg
0917-2   The Battle of Lookout Mountain
0918-0   Encounter at Cold Harbor
0919-9   Fire Over Atlanta
0920-2   Bring the Boys Home

Follow good friends Leah Carter and Jeff Majors as they experience danger, intrigue, compassion, and love in these civil war adventures. Ages 10-14

MOODY
The Name You Can Trust
1-800-678-8812   www.MoodyPress.org

"Too Smart" Jones

4025-8 Pool Party Thief
4026-6 Buried Jewels
4027-4 Disappearing Dogs
4028-2 Dangerous Woman
4029-0 Stranger in the Cave
4030-4 Cat's Secret
4031-2 Stolen Bicycle
4032-0 Wilderness Mystery
4033-9 Spooky Mansion
4034-7 Mysterious Artist

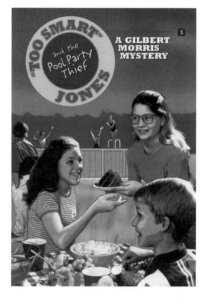

Come along for the adventures and mysteries Juliet "Too Smart" Jones always manages to find. She and her other homeschool friends solve these great adventures and learn biblical truths along the way. Ages 9-14

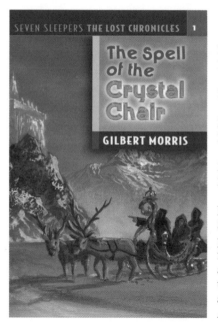

Seven Sleepers - The Lost Chronicles

3667-6   The Spell of the Crystal Chair
3668-4   The Savage Game of Lord Zarak
3669-2   The Strange Creatures of Dr. Korbo
3670-6   City of the Cyborgs
3671-4   The Temptations of Pleasure Island
3672-2   Victims of Nimbo
3673-0   The Terrible Beast of Zor

More exciting adventures from the Seven Sleepers. As these exciting young people attempt to faithfully follow Goel, they learn important moral and spiritual lessons. Come along with them as they encounter danger, intrigue, and mystery.
Ages 10-14

MOODY
The Name You Can Trust
1-800-678-8812 www.MoodyPress.org

Moody Press, a ministry of the Moody Bible Institute,
is designed for education, evangelization, and edification.
If we may assist you in knowing more about Christ
and the Christian life, please write us without obligation:
Moody Press, c/o MLM, Chicago, Illinois 60610.